FOSSIL ROCKS

A novel by

Barbara J. Olexer

Joyous Publishing
Columbia, Maryland, U.S.A.

ISBN 978-0-9722740-7-4

Joyous Publishing
5662 Stevens Forest Road
Suite 136
Columbia, MD 21045-3327
www.joyouspub.com

Printed in the U.S.A.

by Barbara J. Olexer

NONFICTION

*The Enslavement of the American Indian
in Colonial Times*

Murder of a Soul: The Story of Captain Jack
(screenplay)

*What Astrology Means to You: A Handbook of
Astrological Terms, Glyphs, and Applications*

FICTION

They Lived Ever After
Death Takes a Flyer
If You Can't Trust Your Uncle Sam
Father to the Man

Fossil is a real place. It is the county seat of Wheeler County, Oregon and is much as described in these pages except for the fictional MacKenzie Mercury and the impact such an operation would have on the region.

All the characters in the book are entirely the product of my imagination and none are taken from life. Any similarity of names is absolutely coincidental.

Chapter 1

It had been a long day bucking hay but, tired as he was, Wesley Callaghan didn't want to go home yet. There was a band playing at The Pastime and he'd been thinking about it the last couple of days. Finally, he could resist no longer; he was still wearing his work clothes when he went in and took a seat at the bar. The jukebox was just finishing a song and the waitress went over and unplugged it. Wesley ordered a beer and drank deeply before turning around to watch a small band file onto the platform and began to fiddle with their instruments and the P.A. equipment. Wesley watched Monte sling the bass guitar strap over his head and adjust the microphone. Good old Monte; didn't look hardly ten years older, getting a little soft maybe. And Barney Stilwell. There he sat amongst his traps, setting out his brushes, making minute changes in the way the drums stood. Wesley'd always liked Barney's drumming style. The other two bandsmen were strangers. A youngster who looked to be Indian was on the keyboard and a big blond kid was on lead guitar. Monte was evidently the vocalist.

Monte scanned the room approvingly. "Well, look at you," he told the crowd. "There's ol' Howard Thomkins! Hey, Howard! When'd they let you out, boy?"

Howard grinned sheepishly. "It was a bum rap. I never in all my life was drunk and disorderly."

The crowd laughed delightedly.

Monte tipped his hat to a beautiful woman sitting at a table with a couple of other women. "Good evening, Miss MacKenzie," he greeted her formally. Then added, aside to the crowd, "Since Yelisa's boss lady of half of Wheeler County, y'all best be on your good behavior tonight."

Yelisa was used to this kidding and called, "More music and less chatter, Monte!"

The crowd laughed and called agreement.

"Yes, ma'am," Monte said. "One, two, three..."

The band picked up the cue and broke into a raucous rendition of a slightly bawdy country rock number. As they played, Monte continued to scan the crowd and finally saw Wesley. Wesley raised his beer in a salute. When the song ended, Monte spoke over the applause, as the dancers returned to their tables.

"We've got us a real live celebrity tonight, folks. Give us a drum roll, Barney."

Barney looked around without spotting Wesley but complied with a long drum roll. Monte made a sweeping gesture toward Wesley.

"Wesley Callaghan!" Monte exclaimed. "Take a bow, Wes."

Wesley stood and raised his hat to the crowd and Monte. The people looked at Wesley and applauded tentatively. The bandsmen stomped and whistled, even the new men being well acquainted with him by reputation.

"Come on up and join us, Wes," urged Monte.

Wesley was incapable of refusing. He wanted more than anything to be on that platform, singing again. He put his beer on the bar and walked up to join the band. He shook hands with Monte and greeted the others.

"What do you want to do?" Monte asked.

Wesley turned and named a song to the band. They nodded and Monte stepped away from the mike. The band played a fast-tempo number and Wesley sang with them as if they'd rehearsed together for weeks. The song had been a big hit for the young Wesley Callaghan and many in the crowd recognized it and, belatedly, him. As they applauded appreciatively, Wesley turned to the band and named a second song. As he sang, he watched Yelisa. The crowd applauded enthusiastically. Wesley raised his arms in a gesture of benediction, turned to thank the band,

3

then left the platform and the bar without another glance.

"Mr. Wesley Callaghan, folks," Monte enthused. "Maybe we can coax him back tomorrow."

As the band struck up another tune, Wesley emerged into the street, which was nearly deserted. He stopped a moment to rub the head of his magnificent collie dog and walked away.

"Come on, Jack," he murmured.

The sound of the music died away behind him as he turned down a side street to his pickup. Wesley held the door for Jack, climbed in and drove out of town.

Jack took his responsibilities very seriously. His main one was to look out for his human. Fortunately, Wesley was relatively sensible, as humans go, and seldom required more than a nudge to alert him to danger, possible or probable. This summer morning Wesley was safely occupied, running the swather around the field, laying the alfalfa out in thin, curving rows. This field adjoined the evergreen forest and was dotted with small islands of rock and miniscule bogs where springs seeped out of the hillside. Jack was amusing himself by trotting around the alfalfa field, investigating the rock piles for varmints.

It was about mid-morning and warming up, with the dry heat of eastern Oregon. Wesley would have to stop soon, before the alfalfa dried out too much. He had parked his white pickup near the gate when he arrived for work before dawn. Everything had been going well, considering the roughness of the field, and Wesley was pleased. Suddenly the machine choked on something. Wesley cut the motor and descended to the ground. Experience told him it was probably a rock or piece of wire caught in the conditioner.

Though he was no longer in his first youth, he walked with the lithe grace of an athlete and there was nothing of seediness in his good looks. Jack noticed that his man had left the machine and ran up in the hope of a pat or even a romp. Wesley took a water jug from his pickup and took a long drink from it. He took a dish from behind the driver's seat and filled it with water. Jack drank, wagging his tail, as Wesley stroked his sleek golden coat.

Taking some tools from the box in the pickup bed, Wesley returned to the swather. He worked for a few minutes, extracting a short length of rusty barbed wire from the conditioner, then returned the tools. He whistled Jack into the cab and drove back to the ranch, to finish the work day in the shop, servicing the combines so they would be ready to go as soon as the wheat was ripe.

Wesley had come to Wheeler County a few days earlier, not with any particular plan or purpose, just drifting. He was a competent worker, one who could turn his hand to many tasks, and he was not averse to hard work. So he had no trouble getting a job wherever he happened to find himself. He'd drifted all over the west and was accepted as a native in six or seven states. If he wasn't quite happy in his transient life, he wasn't unhappy, either.

Wheeler is one of Oregon's least populated counties and it has only two industries, ranching and mining. It had timber at one time but the sawmill had first been moved to neighboring Morrow County, then closed altogether. Wheeler is a dry county, not in the sense that no liquor is sold, rather the reverse, in fact. But the rainfall is scant. In some parts of the county there is only enough rain to raise a crop of wheat every other year – the land has to lie fallow for a year to store enough moisture to germinate the seed. Other parts of the county are forested and watered by creeks that wind through shady glens and lush meadows.

Wesley called it a day at about the same time the end-of-shift whistle blew at MacKenzie Mercury. Yelisa MacKenzie, Tom Plank, and several other miners rode the elevator to the top of the mine shaft and stepped out. As she and Tom walked to the office, Yelisa smiled and called goodnights to the men who were preparing to leave for the day.

Yelisa looked younger than she was with her slender figure and lovely face. There was a glamour about her that belied her passion for her work. She had an air of confidence and good humor; ever since she had been a little girl, Yelisa's one ambition had been to succeed her father as CEO of MacKenzie Mercury. The autumn after she graduated from the Colorado School of Mines, she had the job forced on her. Both her parents had been killed when they struck a patch of black ice and plunged into the John Day River. Yelisa had thrown herself into the work, grieving for her parents and wishing that she'd been given more time to prepare but reveling in her ability to do it.

Yelisa and Tom were both wearing the dark blue coveralls that MacKenzie Mercury kept for the workmen and visitors to the mine. Yelisa was carrying a bright red sample of cinnabar.

Tom Plank was middle-aged, medium height and stockily built, passably attractive with light brown hair and eyes. He frowned at the ore sample in Yelisa's hand and at the miner who called good night to her.

"Good night, Will," she replied.

The mine and plant employed nearly eighty people, nine of whom worked in the office – engineers, bookkeepers, and secretaries. As Yelisa and Tom were about to enter the building, they heard a rumbling sound and then the ground quaked. Yelisa shook her head. The powder man was getting careless blasting the next day's ore loose.

"Too much powder, Tom," Yelisa said. "Tell Merryman to cut back."

"Sounds okay to me," he said.

"Check it out and make sure."

"Okay, you're the boss." He looked at the ore in her hand again. "What about that drift on the tenth level?"

Yelisa looked down at the bright red rock. "It's rich enough, Tom. But it'll mean putting in another ventilating shaft."

"I don't think so, Yelisa. We can expand the fan system."

"Just moving the air around isn't enough. It's a hundred and four degrees on that level and we need to bring in the cooler outside air."

The office was deserted, the machines were quiet, and the phones were silent. They entered Yelisa's private office and removed the protective clothing and hard hats, putting the protective coveralls in a covered hamper. Yelisa was wearing her usual work clothes of jeans, shirt, and boots. Tom wore slacks and an open-necked white shirt and boots.

Yelisa propped one hip on her desk and Tom took the cinnabar and put it in a glass case with a lot of other rocks.

"It'll cost more," Tom said.

"I know it."

"It'll slow production, too. We've got twice as many orders coming in now than we had six months ago. If we're going to fill them, we'll have to get the ore out faster."

"There are better ways," Yelisa said. "Put a crew to work on that ventilating shaft Monday." She moved to a huge wall chart and pointed as she spoke. "It will run through the clay and gravel but we'll miss that outcropping of shale. We'll hire a second shift and get twice the goodwill of the crew."

"Miners are a dime a dozen."

"An experienced, loyal crew is money in the bank, Tom." She eyed him quizzically. "I've got to run now, I'm meeting Roger and Pam Elwood for dinner and they're only here for the evening."

"See you tomorrow."

Yelisa nodded and strode out to her car, a black Mercedes. She reflected that Tom was not shaping as well as she'd thought he would when she hired him a year ago. He seemed to be more interested in making an impression on her than in his work. He wasn't very good at impressing her or he would know by now how she felt about her employees.

Fossil is the seat of Wheeler County. Fully two-thirds of the population live in the town and most of them were on the main street that Friday night as Wesley and Jack walked from the café to the Pastime. Townspeople, ranchers, and miners

9

had all come out looking for relaxation and entertainment. The crowd was centered around the two main buildings – Dightman's Hotel and the Fossil Pastime. Dightman's was a white frame house, three stories tall, which qualified it as one of Wheeler County's two skyscrapers. The other was the Court House. Dightman's dining room was the only place in town that served meals in a leisurely, quiet way.

The main street made a right-angle turn halfway through town and almost all the businesses were located on the one street. It was an old town, the newest buildings being at least thirty years old, the oldest dating from the 1870s. The crowd was dressed in jeans and western shirts for the most part. Wesley had changed clothes after work but the only difference from his working garb was their freshness and the shirt being unbuttoned halfway to his waist.

As he progressed along the street, Wesley greeted no one, smiled at no one. As far as he was concerned, he and Jack might have been alone in Fossil. A couple of the women he met eyed him approvingly and one turned to watch him for a moment. Wesley apparently noticed only the posters in shop windows advertising the Wheeler County Fair and Rodeo scheduled to take place the last weekend of July. Wesley commanded Jack to stay outside the Pastime door and the collie sat obediently as his man went inside.

Again Wesley chose a barstool near the band platform and ordered a beer. When the bartender brought it, he turned to face the room, watching the crowd. He was excited to see Monte and Barney again and happy that they were doing well. Fossil was not the big time for musicians but small-town America was a lot of fun to play for. The people were generally friendly and the money, while not princely, was more than merely adequate. Wesley was suddenly impatient for the juke box to be turned off and the band to arrive for their set. He hadn't seen Monte for years, not since he'd split that night in L.A., leaving Monte and the band on their own. All at once an overpowering nostalgia swept over him. He wanted to rush into the dressing room, or whatever a place like the Pastime called a dressing room, seize a guitar and control of the band, and play all night.

Memories crowded his mind: barrooms thick with smoke; concert stages set up in sports arenas; girls screaming and tearing at his clothes; and the music. The music that was at once the cause and the effect. His music. Days on the beach strumming out new melodies, nights in the studio arranging and recording.

Wesley had played many times since the night he'd left the band that he and Monte had put together but he'd never experienced this fierce uprush of longing before. He knew he wouldn't be able to withstand it. Somehow he'd have to

11

join Monte on the platform, he'd perform with the band one more time, come hell or high water. He forced himself to sit on the barstool and drink his beer as if his emotions were not in total chaos.

Yelisa had met Pam and Roger Elwood at Dightman's and they'd enjoyed a good steak dinner. Pam was a little tiresome – Yelisa often wondered what Roger found to admire in her. Clothes and decorating seemed to be all the woman knew anything about. Yelisa had had to fight down the impulse to brain her with the wine bottle in the seventh minute of a description of Pam's search for exactly the right shade of blue for the living room carpet. Yelisa hadn't done much decorating except for her new suite. She'd had two bedrooms in the old Victorian mansion she'd inherited remodeled into her private sitting room. When the carpenters were about finished, she'd gone to Portland for a couple of days, checked out some of the better furniture stores, picked one with a clerk she liked and left her order. There'd been a lot of swatches, she remembered, and she'd chosen a couple of shades of green. She had a list of the furniture she wanted, another of room dimensions and window sizes. It had taken a day and a half and her bedroom, bath, and sitting room suited her perfectly. She couldn't understand how it could take Pam Elwood six months of apparently incessant hostilities between herself and the salespeople of several stores and shops to get one carpet right.

In keeping with local custom, Yelisa and the Elwoods were dressed in jeans and western shirts. Yelisa wore a carved leather belt with a big square silver trophy buckle. Technically correctly dressed, Pam and Roger missed looking natural; they looked like people in costume.

As they sipped liqueurs and coffee, Roger reverted to the beginning of the conversation, which concerned his company's purchase of mercury.

"What do you think, Yelisa? Can you get me the extra flasks?"

"I don't think we'll have any problem with it, Roger. I've decided to put on a double shift."

"Well, that's a relief. We were afraid that with the demand up, we might have to stand in line."

"MacKenzie Mercury doesn't do business like that. The price is up because of the increased demand, but our old customers are still first on the delivery list."

Pam felt she'd already suffered enough business talk. "I don't see how you can bear to talk nothing but business all the time. Especially you, Yelisa. Don't you ever relax?"

"Look, sweetheart," her mate explained resignedly, "it's the other way around. We talk business because we like to. We relax when we have to."

Yelisa had no wish to witness an argument or a fit of sulks so she smiled placatingly. "Pam's right, Roger. If you're finished, let's go over and give the Pastime a whirl. There's a great little band playing there."

Pam's eyes lighted up. "Oh, let's. I saw a poster in that dreary little store that Monte Alvarez and his band are playing. I love country rock."

The three of them gathered up their Stetsons – the women's had silver ornaments pinned to the crowns – and Pam slung her purse over her shoulder. Yelisa pulled a roll of bills out of her pocket and laid some in the little leather folder that held the check.

The Pastime was nearly full when Yelisa and the Elwoods entered but Yelisa spotted a vacant table at the edge of the small dance floor. A waitress dressed in jeans and a black t-shirt with a silver Pastime emblazoned across the chest hurried up to take their order. Several couples were dancing to the juke box and Pam and Roger joined them. Yelisa surveyed the room, nodding to acquaintances and smiling and waving at her friends. Several people called greetings to her. Wesley noticed her as soon as she entered the room and when her glance reached him, their eyes met and held in that extra couple of seconds that make a glance significant. Yelisa looked away first and Wesley added that to the turmoil within himself.

Chapter 2

Trudy Allen was lying in bed. She was feeling very lonesome and forlorn. Wesley had come in shortly after six, showered and changed, eaten a little and gone out again, taking Jack with him. Trudy was a city girl, well, perhaps not a girl, she was slightly past thirty. But she'd seldom been out of L.A., never before for longer than a week. Finding herself wandering around Nevada and Oregon with Wesley, fetching up on this ranch miles and miles from anywhere, she was frightened. And, to add to her fears, Wesley had begun to change.

In their first weeks together, he'd been kind and considerate. Never much for laughing, he'd been charming and debonair. Not that he was exactly unkind now. Trudy saw no meanness in Wesley. It was just that he was moody, even more silent than usual. Like tonight. He'd gone out, without telling her where he was going or how long he'd be gone. In the early days of their relationship he'd taken her with him when he went out in the evenings, usually to a bar or, when they'd been in Winnemucca, to a small casino where they'd had a few drinks, gambled a

15

little at the 21 tables and sometimes even danced. Wesley was a wonderful dancer. Trudy smiled a little at the recollection.

She'd thought she was extraordinarily lucky when Wesley came into her life. He'd seemed so safe, open-handed and steady. Well, steady in that he didn't ask her to sign up for destitution checks at every welfare office they passed. No, as far as money went, Wesley was perfectly adequate and very generous. Adequate in other ways, too. And handsome. Trudy enjoyed his love-making, liked the way his arms felt around her, the way his strength enfolded her.

But why was he changing? Had she done something to upset him? Surely he couldn't be tired of her already? She looked around the room. It was clean, almost painfully clean and tidy to her thinking. She had found in the first few days they were together that Wesley insisted on clean surroundings. Left to herself, Trudy tended to be a casual housekeeper. All right, she admitted to herself, a slob. So what? But Wesley wouldn't stand for a dirty house. So she took pains to keep the place clean. Not that it was much of a place. Three rooms comprised the entire cottage which had been built about fifty years earlier for a ranch hand with no family. Kitchen, living room, bedroom and bath. The furniture was as old as the house.

Trudy reflected that it couldn't be her cooking, either. Although she wasn't much of a cook, Wesley wasn't much of an eater. He liked a substantial lunch but breakfast and dinner were often skipped altogether or merely a glass of milk or a few bites of whatever was handy. He took vitamins and minerals religiously, but he wasn't much interested in food.

She glanced complacently into the mirror tilted down over the dresser. The change in Wesley couldn't be attributed to any lack of charm in her person. Her hair was a rich glossy brown and her complexion was clear and rosy. She stirred uneasily and ran her hands reassuringly over the curves of her waist. No, her figure was still fine. The semi-transparent red nightie was cut very low in front and fell only to her hips, revealing a voluptuous body, ripe and promising.

Trudy had been reading a paperback romance but she'd thrown it down beside her on the bed as she tried to think what Wesley's change of attitude meant and what might have caused it. As she puzzled, she heard a car or pickup coming. She knew it was Wesley coming home, but what if it wasn't? The cottage was situated at the end of a long lane, away from the main ranch buildings so the hand who occupied it could keep an eye out for trespassers, coyotes, or whatever. The city girl sat up and listened apprehensively. The vehicle pulled up beside the house and stopped. A door slammed and the kitchen door opened and closed. Trudy watched the bedroom doorway, her eyes wide, her breath coming quickly and shallowly. Footsteps crossed the kitchen, approached the bedroom.

The dark rectangle of the doorway suddenly and silently framed Wesley's body. His face was in shadow so that Trudy recognized him more by his clothes than his features. He stepped into the light and looked unsmilingly at Trudy. He began to unsnap his shirt. Trudy was relieved, although she had been sure, really, that it was Wesley. And, at the same time, she wasn't relieved. The tension between them still held.

"Wesley," she breathed. "You startled me. Where've you been all this time, honey?"

Wesley didn't bother to answer. He'd known from the first that Trudy's conversational talents were negligible. He had tried to be polite for a little while but that only encouraged her to talk. He often failed to answer, not to be rude but to spare himself the boredom of listening. He continued to undress in silence.

"Have a good time? I wish you'd taken me with you. I'm totally sick of being cooped up in this place. No TV, no neighbors, no…"

Wesley tuned her out and got into bed. He was nearly asleep when Trudy, still very wide awake, spoke. His face was turned away from her but she was lying on her side, turned toward him. She needed his warmth, his caring. She was terribly afraid she wasn't going to get it.

"Wesley?" she said softly. When he didn't answer, she spoke more firmly. "Wesley."

"Yeah."

"I'm pregnant." She didn't know how else to say it so it came out flat and bald. It got his attention. He sat up, suddenly wide awake, and looked down at her dourly.

"Nonsense," he said.

Trudy sat up. "It's true." She hesitated, then asked, "What are we going to do?"

Wesley was frightened and, being frightened, he was harsher with her than he meant to be. "We? It's not my baby."

Trudy was near tears. "You know there's been no one else, Wesley."

"Not since we met, maybe. But how about before?"

"I was afraid you wouldn't accept the responsibility. But you have to know the baby's yours."

There was a long pause before Wesley asked, "When was your last period?"

Trudy began to cry. Although she'd been pretty sure he would react in just this way, it was a blow to her. She'd hoped that he would accept the baby and herself. She'd hoped that, although they didn't love each other, they could be a family, make a home. It was that hope that had kept her from announcing her pregnancy earlier, while abortion would have been the obvious answer. She didn't want the child but she had

19

hoped that she would be taken care of through the baby. She was very tired of moving from man to man, building nothing, sharing nothing but sex. She longed for security and that nebulous contentment that takes the place of happiness for so many people.

"You're so cold, Wes. I don't know what to say to make you believe me."

Wesley looked at her, his face expressionless. She looked up at him and buried her face in a handful of tissues, weeping bitterly.

"Now that I think about it, you haven't had any periods since we've been together, have you?"

She couldn't argue, knew he wouldn't be deceived. But maybe he would respond to an appeal to his honor, his compassion. She choked down her sobs and dried her eyes. "Wesley…"

He interrupted coldly. "And I've been very, very careful. It's not my baby, Trudy."

Yelisa slept badly that night, an unusual thing for her. As she tossed and pummeled her pillow, she saw Wesley Callaghan. She mentally caressed his fine, strong body; she imagined his lips on hers. She pushed the image away to concentrate on some problem at the mine or plant only to find herself wondering if his eyes were blue or gray.

She turned on the light and went into the sitting room. She put some music on and wished she had some of Wesley's recordings. Music was important to her and while she was in high school and college she had been a member of various small bands. She knew her voice was good and various people had told her that she should pursue a singing career but her dream had always been to run MacKenzie Mercury. Her music collection included a couple of hundred tapes, CDs, and records. Her taste could be called eclectic but eccentric was probably a better word. She had everything from her mother's Bing Crosby records to Dwight Yoakum to classical symphonies. She put on one of her favorite symphonies. Yelisa didn't drink much but she went to a small refrigerator that was concealed in a cabinet and poured a wine spritzer. She pulled the atlas off the shelf and put it on the coffee table. As she sipped, she opened the atlas and began to find places that she intended to visit someday. Bread Loaf, Vermont. Giltedge, Montana. Volcano, California.

Yelisa had never been married but she'd had a few relationships. She'd been reasonably popular in high school. Which wasn't much of a trick since there were only sixteen people in her class and about the same number in the others. But when your family employs at least one parent of most of your admirers, it's hard to take the admiration seriously. In college she'd been too concentrated on grooming herself to take over the operation of MacKenzie Mercury some day to allow herself to become seriously involved. Since then she simply hadn't cared to take the time or spare the energy to cope with marriage.

Wesley's face came between her and the atlas. From the way he'd looked at her, he was not totally indifferent. He had seemed to find her attractive. His jeans fit perfectly. She thought of his shoulders, wide and strong. He hadn't smiled at her. Come to think of it, he hadn't smiled at all. She wondered what he was doing in Fossil. Why had he joined the band to sing those two numbers? Obviously he and the band knew each other. At least he and Monte knew each other. Had he sang the second song to her? He had certainly looked at her as he sang it. At the time it had seemed like he was singing to her. Maybe she had imagined it. She had a good imagination.

Soon after Monte and the boys began this gig, she had become acquainted with them, especially with Monte. She had even sung with them a few times after people told him she was talented. She didn't understand how anyone could bear to travel like they did instead of having a solid, steady base and a home three generations old. It was nearly dawn before she was tired enough to sleep. She curled up on the couch and the next morning she didn't remember dreaming at all. At least not dreaming in her sleep.

Wesley began work on a new field the next morning. He didn't even bother to cuss when he hit another chunk of barbed wire about eight o'clock. The day was hot, even as early as that, and he was stripped to the waist, working at getting the wire out when an old blue Dodge pickup rattled over the dirt road and into the field. It pulled up by the swather and Wesley straightened up and nodded at his boss. Burt Radzinski was a little round man, tubby and double-chinned. He'd been working the ranch founded by his great-grandfather for nearly fifty years and couldn't imagine living anywhere else.

"How bad is it?" he asked, gesturing at the machine.

Wesley shrugged. "Just a piece of wire. I'll have her going in a few minutes."

Radzinski nodded. "Okay. Think you can finish this field today?"

Wesley looked around. "Barring more wire, I think so. If I do, what do you want me to do tomorrow?"

"Hell, man, tomorrow's Sunday. There's nothing urgent enough to start on Sunday. Monday you can ride out to Lava Flat and fix that fence on the north side. My cattle have been straying through and old Jessom'll be sending me a bill for forage."

"All right."

Wesley returned to work and Radzinski whipped the pickup around and rattled off.

Having slept badly the night before, Yelisa was inclined to be a little short with Tom when they met in her office Saturday afternoon for a conference that lasted until evening. They discussed the plans he'd drawn up for the second shift, and the ventilating shaft in detail. Yelisa sat behind her desk and Tom took the visitor's chair facing her.

She tossed a sheaf of papers onto the desk. "That's it, Tom. Go ahead and get a second shift organized."

"Right. But. I don't know, Yelisa. Are you sure there's enough demand? What if Wyrick Chemical cancels their order? Or some of the others do? What if the demand doesn't hold steady? We'll be left holding the bag and it's mighty damned expensive."

She spoke impatiently. "We've been through all that. Let me worry about financing and demand. You just find the crew and get the flasks ready to ship."

Tom was unconvinced but, after all, she was the boss. "All right. I'll start first thing Monday morning."

Yelisa nodded and rose. "Good night, Tom," she said as she left the room.

"Good night."

Yelisa went straight from her office to the Pastime. She had phoned to reserve a table and it was waiting for her. She ordered a Perrier with a twist of lemon and applauded politely as Monte and the band finished a set. The crowd was larger than the night before and a little rowdier.

Monte held up one hand. "Thank you, folks. Thank you. The band and I will be back in just fifteen minutes. So get your dancin' shoes on, we gonna boogie tonight!"

The band came down from the platform and Yelisa called to Monte. He looked around and she waved at him.

"Monte! Come over here."

He joined her and the waitress brought him a beer without waiting for him to order it. He thanked her and took a deep draught. Someone started the juke box and a number of couples crowded the dance floor.

"Well, lady, what can I do you for?"

Yelisa grinned at him. "I want a favor, Monte."

He grinned back. "Well, now, I can't hardly think of anything I'd rather do than a favor for you."

"Tell me about Wesley Callaghan."

Monte leaned back and looked at her specutively. "Wes and I go back a long way. I first met him more than twenty years ago when I was workin' in Bakersfield, just gettin' started. He had a group and we used to jam together. Then we merged the two groups and featured Wesley's singing."

"He's good."

Monte looked at her sharply. "He's good, all right. If he wanted to, he could record in platinum."

"Well, why doesn't he?"

"I'll tell you the truth, Yelisa. I don't know. We cut a dozen sides and nine of them hit the charts. Five went gold and now that they're on a CD, they've gone platinum. For a couple of years we toured and broke attendance records at half the places we played."

"When was that?"

"Our last tour was sixteen years ago. One day Wes said he'd had enough and walked. Next I heard he was buckin' hay on a ranch in Nevada."

"Yeah, that was my next question. What's he doing in Fossil?"

"I don't know. Working for some rancher, most likely. I got to go." Monte stood, looking down at her earnestly. "Listen, don't get involved. I love him like a brother but as far as women are concerned, he's bad news."

Yelisa smiled up at him. "Um-hm. Thanks, Monte."

He looked at her exasperatedly and shook his head as he went back up on the platform where the band was ready to begin the next set. They played a couple of recent country-rock hits and the crowd was very enthusiastic. Wesley walked in and found a stool at the end of the bar near the platform. Yelisa glanced at him, looked away resolutely but, laughing inwardly at herself, kept glancing back at him. He was certainly a fine-looking man. Wesley sipped his beer and watched the band. The song ended and Monte gestured at Wesley.

"Well, look a-here, folks. Wesley Callaghan! Say, Wes, you ain't too tired after a long, hard day's work to come on up here and sing for us, are you?"

Wesley acknowledged the applause, put his beer down on the bar and stepped onto the platform.

He spoke to Monte. "Can I borrow a guitar?"

Monte got one from the back of the platform and Wesley strummed a few chords experimentally. He spoke to the band and they struck up a love song. As he sang, Wesley's eyes kept straying to meet Yelisa's. He sang another and before the applause died completely away, Monte stepped to the mike and demanded that Yelisa come up and sing with them. Wesley was astonished but readily joined in urging her to come up to the mike.

The crowd loved it and they applauded and yelled their approval. Rather surprised at her own eagerness, Yelisa hopped up onto the platform and grinned at the audience, then at the band.

"Okay," she said into the mike, "you asked for it." She looked around at the band and named the song she would sing.

The audience applauded and Wesley offered her his guitar. She smiled and shook her head. The band launched into the intro and Yelisa began to sing.

Wesley strummed along, knowing the song and also knowing that whatever he was doing didn't really matter right at the moment. This girl was good. She was really good. He had to know her, to know all about her. Especially why she lived in Fossil instead of L.A. or Nashville.

Yelisa sang a second song but declined to sing another. Waving her appreciation at the crowd and the band, she returned to her table.

Wesley sang one more song then, as the applause rolled over him in waves, he handed the guitar back to Monte, raised his arms in farewell, left the platform and strode to the door, looking neither right nor left. He stopped just outside the door to rub Jack's head before walking through the sparse foot traffic to Filson's Motel at one end of the main street. He and Jack went into room six.

Chapter 3

Monte's suite – bedroom, bath, and combination kitchen-living room – at Dightman's Hotel was on the second floor. It was nearly noon and Monte was just out of bed, preparing to take a shower, when there was a knock at the door. He hastily wrapped a towel around his waist and flung the door open. To his delight, Wesley stood on the threshold.

"Come on in, boy."

"You had breakfast?" Wesley asked, stepping inside and shutting the door behind him.

"Breakfast? I haven't hardly got up yet, Wes."

"You are a little what they call dishabille. Go on and get dressed and I'll buy you breakfast."

"I was just about to jump in the shower."

"Well, go on and jump. I'll just mess around with this guitar while I'm waiting. If that's all right."

Monte waved comprehensively around the room. "Oh, sure. Help yourself. Hell, Wes, you know that."

Wesley picked up the guitar with an eagerness he couldn't conceal and stroked the wood, enjoying the touch of the polished surface. He strummed it tentatively. Monte retired into the bathroom, grinning.

Thirty minutes later the two men were in the dining room with plates of bacon and eggs.

"Who are the new guys?" Wesley asked.

"Gary Radner – he's on guitar – and Jimmy Butler on keyboards."

"They play the old arrangements just like we used to."

"Yeah, sometimes it's downright uncanny."

"You aren't workin' tonight, are you?"

"Nope."

"I got my pickup outside. Come on and we'll head out in the mountains. I'll show you some of the most beautiful scenery in the world."

"I thought you'd glommed the most beautiful scenery in the world last night. And the night before."

"The blond. Yeah. She is surely something special."

Monte grinned. "She is that."

"Who is she? She lives here, doesn't she?"

"Yes, she does. And before you do me any favors under the impression that I'm going to introduce you to her, let me tell you that I told her you're strictly bad news for women."

Wesley was amused. "You did? Thanks, Monte."

Monte was taken aback. "Thanks? For what?"

"Well, you just told me that she asked about me. And that you told her I'm bad news. That, together with my native charm, ought to make me pretty near irresistible."

Monte scowled, then laughed. "It will, won't it? I'll be damned."

The two men stopped on their way out of town to pick up a cold pack of beer at Isbister's General Store. Wesley drove up Fossil Hill to the summit where the barren hillsides gave way abruptly to forested slopes and the hill became Kinzua Mountain. They drove through Kinzua, once a thriving, bustling lumber mill town, now not even a ghost town. The company had moved operations and sold the buildings so that all that remained was the ruined foundations of the commercial buildings. Red poppies and blue bachelor buttons were scattered where the houses used to be and the superintendent's ruined garden had a few straggling shrubs and rock walls left. They took an old logging road that had once been graveled out of Kinzua but presently left it for an old dirt road that took them into the high timber. Jack sat on the seat between them, watching the scenery as they bumped along. They saw few a cattle but no wild animals.

Wesley broke the long silence. "You didn't tell me her name."

"I'm not sure I'm going to."

"It's real flattering that you think I'm such hell on wheels with women that it's dangerous for me to even know their names."

Monte grinned at him. "All right. Her name's Yelisa MacKenzie and she runs MacKenzie Mercury."

Wesley whistled soundlessly. "Big time, huh?"

"She's a nice woman, Wes, let her alone."

Wesley glanced at Monte then looked straight ahead down the road. He forded a shallow creek and rounded a curve. Before them loomed a cliff which offered a magnificent view of the surrounding forest. Wesley parked as far off the road as he could and stepped outside, snapping his fingers for Jack. Monte stepped out and stretched luxuriously.

"This is definitely one of your better ideas, Wes. It's sure a whole different world from barrooms all night and sleeping all day."

"Come on."

Wesley led the way up a steep trail to the top of the cliff with Jack frisking around them as they climbed. The mountains rose in huge folds, stretching before them as far as they could see. Flats and meadows dotted the thickly growing forest and the creek tumbled down the hill beside the cliff and sparkled across the woods at their feet.

Monte was puffing a little as they reached the top. "You want a job, Wes?"

"I've got a job."

"Doin' what? Farmin'?"

"Ranching."

"Damn it, Wes, a guy that has music in him like you got – he owes it to himself, to the world, to do something with that talent. Hell's bells, man, anybody can farm!"

"Ranch."

"All right, ranch! You come back with me and the boys and in a year we'll all be on top again."

"On top of what? Listen to yourself. You're so winded you can hardly talk. It's you that needs a change of occupation. You're gettin' soft. No exercise."

"Yeah, I know it." Monte patted his little paunch ruefully. "I keep meaning to get with the program but I keep putting it off."

Wesley threw a playful punch at his stomach. "Well, don't put it off too long, son."

Wesley turned and strode down the mountainside. Monte and Jack followed. They were silent most of the way back to Fossil. Monte was wondering if he'd better let Wesley alone to cogitate on the idea of re-joining the band or whether it wouldn't be better to follow up his advantage. If he had an advantage. Wesley was thinking how good the guitar had felt in his hands and wondering whether he hadn't better go back to his music before he ruined his touch working as a ranch hand.

He knew he still had a lot to say with music, snatches of melody and bits of lyrics ran through his head constantly. He had a number of completed songs that he hadn't published as yet. It had given him a certain pleasure to know that they were his and no other ear had ever heard them; no other voice had ever sung them; no other hands had ever played them. It amused him when he realized that he seemed to feel about his music much as he had felt about his first love.

Women, he thought. Women were the devil and all. He'd have to get shut of Trudy. Tonight would be as good a time as any, he supposed. How he hated those scenes. They always ended the same way – tears and recriminations. He hadn't told a woman he loved her, hadn't made a commitment to a woman since he and Gayle had split up nearly twenty years ago. After the split, sex had become totally casual. He'd always steered clear of teeny-boppers but the groupies had been fun. Everybody understood the rules and nobody got hurt. Then there'd been a long succession of women like Trudy. Not really relationships; more like a string of one night stands with the same partner.

He was surprised to find himself thinking it would be great to find someone to care about and settle down with her. He wondered if it was too late. Could a woman mean enough to him to make him want to commit to her? Marriage? Could marriage be fun? Or interesting?

Permanent? Wesley didn't know but he thought maybe it was time to find out. It was definitely time for a change in his life. Maybe he would re-join the band.

As they drove into Fossil, Wesley and Monte were singing an old hit song. They gave it a big finish as Wesley pulled up in front of Dightman's.

"'Night, Monte. Tell her I work for Burt Radzinski and I'll be at Lava Flat tomorrow."

"The hell is I will!"

Monte stepped out of the pickup as Wesley answered.

"I think you will."

Monte slammed the door shut and started up the walk. Wesley drove away.

When he got to the cottage, Trudy was sitting on the sagging old sofa waiting for him. He told her gently that they were through and withstood her tantrum as patiently as he could. He got his suitcase from the closet and began to pack. Trudy sat on the side of the bed and wept noisily.

"But why, Wesley? I just don't understand. How can you leave me like this? Just walk out after dragging me away up here where I don't know anyone?"

Damn, he thought. He might have known Trudy would use that weapon against him. Well, it had worked after a fashion when he was younger but it had been some time since he'd allowed a woman to lay a guilt trip on him for something she'd eagerly cooperated in.

"Back up," he said. "I didn't drag you anywhere. You wanted to come and you came. Now I want to go and I'm going."

He went into the bathroom and rummaged in the medicine cabinet, returning with a double handful of toiletries and vitamins.

"But, Wes. I don't have any money. I have nowhere to go, no one to turn to. You have to take care of me."

Wesley went on packing. "No. You have to take care of yourself."

He snapped the bag shut and pulled a roll of bills out of his pocket. He peeled off most of it and tossed it on the bed beside her.

Trudy threw the money at him angrily. "I don't want your money!"

She fought for control and dried her tears. She went to him and put her arms around him, smiling up at him as she pressed her body against his.

"After all we've been to each other, Wes?"

He looked down at her, remote and unresponsive. He gently disentangled himself from her embrace and picked up the bag.

"We haven't been much to each other, Trudy. Just an easy lay for both of us."

Trudy began to weep again. "I thought you cared for me. I thought we'd settle down and get married."

Wesley almost smiled. "Did you?"

"I'm going to have your baby," she cried desperately. "You can't leave me here, penniless and alone."

Wesley pointed at the money on the floor. "You're not penniless – there's plenty there to get you back to L.A. and your sister's. You can't stay here anyhow; Mr. Radzinski will need the house for another hand."

"You're cold, Wes," Trudy cried. "You're icy cold clear through. You don't even care about your own baby."

He walked to the door and turned. "It's not my baby."

He went out through the kitchen, snapped his fingers for Jack, and left.

Trudy stood looking after him, tears streaming down her face. "I'll make you pay," she gritted.

Wesley spent a bad night at Filson's Motel. He felt sorry for Trudy but it was an impersonal sorrow, like what people feel for earthquake victims half a world away. He hadn't caused Trudy's problems; she wasn't any worse off for having known him. But, he thought ruefully, she wasn't any better off either. He thought back over the weeks they'd been together, trying to be sure that the baby she said she was carrying was not his. In the end, he was certain it was not. He was disgusted with himself to find that he was thinking of Yelisa MacKenzie, wondering if he'd read her psychology right and if she'd be at Lava Flat the next day. Off with the old, on with the new, he thought. Wesley Callaghan, you really are no damn good. He began to plan the picnic he would take in case she should show up around noon. The cook at the café would put it up for him, she seemed to be glad to fix his food just the way he liked it.

It was late when Wesley got up Monday morning. He secured the picnic and it was nearly eight when he arrived at Radzinski's barn to saddle the bay mare. The flat was accessible by road but it was bad and wound around so much that it was quicker to ride. Besides, there was heavy brush in that area and no telling how much of the fence would need repairs. It was nearly noon when Wesley began work on the big break. The barbed wire was down, all three strands of it, and badly rusted. He'd have to splice in some new wire. He got the little roll he'd brought and pulled the burlap away. One end sprang loose and whipped across his thigh. He was very glad that he'd put his chaps on. He'd got the first strand spliced and back in place when nature called.

He put the fence-building tool in his back pocket and walked over to a huge lava slab that hung out over a steep slope a little distance away. He stripped off his leather gloves as he walked and pushed them into the other back pocket. He was standing there, relieving himself, when he heard someone pushing through the brush.

Yelisa spoke, walking up behind him. "It's beautiful country, isn't it?"

Wesley looked over his shoulder, mentally uttered an obscene word, congratulated himself on knowing her psychology, mentally uttered another obscene word and answered, "Yes, ma'am."

"I saw your horse back there so I left mine and walked up."

"Good of you to come."

All at once it dawned on Yelisa that he was keeping his back to her for a reason. She flushed and turned away, walking rapidly back toward her horse. Wesley did some more mental cussing and followed her, still pulling on his zipper. He caught up with her and Jack trotted up to join them, wagging his tail happily.

"Hold on a minute," Wesley said. "You didn't ride clear up here just to turn around the second you got here, did you?"

Yelisa showed her temper then. She might be deep in the throes of infatuation but she still had her pride. "What do you mean, ride clear up here? If you think I rode up here to see you, think again."

She kept on walking.

"Yes, ma'am. I haven't had my lunch yet. There's a real pleasant spot just over there by the creek. I'd be pleased if you'd join me."

Yelisa stopped and looked him full in the face. She saw nothing but the polite look of an acquaintance who was trying to help her over an embarrassing moment and just a glint of suppressed humor. She threw her head back and laughed.

"All right. It isn't often that I fall into playing games but I was surprised."

"So was I," Wesley said fervently.

Yelisa laughed again and they walked together to the horses. She frankly watched him as he removed his chaps, left the fence-building tool and his gloves in the saddlebag and took out a substantial lunch package. They walked down to the creek to a shady, grassy spot. He tossed the package on the ground and continued to the creek where he stretched out at full length on the bank and washed his face and hands, drinking deeply of the cold, clear water. Yelisa hunkered down to wash her hands and drink.

Wesley started to rise and their eyes met. He leaned toward her and she expected to be kissed. Instead he abruptly pulled her to her feet. She pressed herself against him. Wesley closed his eyes for a moment then took her by the hand and led her to the picnic. Yelisa stood watching him as he sat, unwrapped the lunch and started to lay out two of everything.

"You were expecting me!" she exclaimed. "Were you expecting me?"

"I thought it was possible you might decide to ride out this way today. I like to be prepared for guests."

Yelisa sat down cross-legged and took a sandwich. "My lord, you're conceited."

Wesley began to peel a hard-cooked egg. "Well, I had a little inside information."

"Monte."

Wesley nodded. "My friend, Monte."

"Mine, too. I had breakfast with him this morning."

Wesley salted the egg and took a bite. Yelisa put her sandwich down.

"Monte breakfasts around ten or eleven most days," he remarked.

"He ate at seven-thirty today."

Wesley stretched out on his side, eating his lunch, looking at Yelisa. Jack laid his head on her knee and she stroked him absently.

"He wants your sandwich," Wesley told her.

"What? Who?"

"Jack. He see it just laying there and he wants it."

"Oh. Is it okay?"

Wesley nodded. "Why are you named Yelisa?"

She pinched off pieces of the sandwich and fed them to Jack. He took them very politely and delicately, being careful not to touch her fingers.

"I was named after my great-grandmother. I think it's Viking or something."

"Most people seem to know all about their ancestors. You're not interested?"

"I can't get into it. They're dead and gone; my interest is in the here and now. I guess I'm selfish."

"Yes, I expect you're selfish. Spoiled, too, being head of such a big mining concern and having power over all the people who work for you. Power almost of life or death."

"Actually, I do have the power of life or death. If I make a wrong decision about the mine, it could cost a lot of lives. You think I'm power hungry?"

"I don't know. Are you?"

"Not until now." She watched Jack wolf down the last bite of the sandwich. "Why don't you pursue your musical career?"

"Will you be at the Pastime tonight?"

"Probably."

"Then I'll begin pursuing tonight."

He gathered up the wrappers and peelings and made a neat package of them. He pulled Yelisa to her feet. She put her arms around his neck but leaned her head back to see his expression. A strong emotion flashed across his face but she couldn't read it.

"I'd purely love to oblige you, ma'am," he drawled. "But Mr. Radzinski is paying me to fix that fence yonder. And I just don't know what he'd say if he found I'd been taking his money for time I spent making love to you."

Yelisa dropped her arms and stepped back, grinning up at him. "I expect I'm making a fool of myself but I don't seem to care. I guess Burt would say I have enough money of my own without him paying for my pleasure."

Wesley spoke with sudden passion. "Are you so sure it would be your pleasure?"

He ran his hand from her waist to her spine and up into her hair. His lips came down on hers demandingly. He stopped as suddenly as he began. He strode to the horses and put on his chaps. Yelisa followed, tightened Firefly's cinch, untied the palomino mare, and by the time she was aboard, Wesley was pulling on his gloves and was halfway to the broken fence.

Yelisa rode slowly down the trail, savoring Wesley's passion, thinking what it meant. That he was undergoing some kind of inner struggle she could see; the nature of the struggle was more difficult to divine. Evidently she was part of it. She couldn't think why, though. But she had what was more or less a date at the Pastime that very evening and she'd best get to work so she'd have the evening free.

She didn't understand why this man had the power to stir her as others had not. She thought about the men she'd dated in college. None were as handsome as Wesley but she'd always valued friendliness, a sense of humor, and cheerfulness above mere good looks. Mere good looks? There was nothing mere about Wesley's looks.

All the way down the mountain she thought of the coming evening with Wesley. By the time she reached her stable and handed the reins over to her hired man, she'd decided that she would not wait for Wesley to make the next move.

Chapter 4

Wesley sat on his usual barstool, turned so he could watch the people at the tables. The Pastime was unusually crowded for a Monday night. Although Yelisa had called him conceited, he really wasn't. It never occurred to him that the crowd was there in the hope that he would be, too. Yelisa had come in late. He'd watched her go straight to the table near the platform where she'd sat Saturday night. He knew then that she'd asked the management to reserve the table for her. The knowledge pleased him very much. Monte looked a question at him and he nodded.

Monte spoke as the applause for the last number died down. "Now, the man you've all been hoping for – Mr. Wesley Callaghan!"

Wesley walked onto the platform, took the guitar Monte handed him and turned to the band, naming one of his old hits. He hardly glanced at Yelisa as he sang. Next he sang right to her, a smoothly sweet love song from years ago. The crowd loved the early tunes and they had caught onto the byplay between Wesley and Yelisa. Few things could have pleased them more than to have a famous entertainer pay attention to their own Yelisa MacKenzie.

As the audience applauded, Wesley handed the guitar back to Monte, saluted the audience and walked out, looking neither right nor left. As the door closed behind him, Yelisa rose and, grinning, waved at the crowd. She followed him outside.

Wesley and Jack were about a block ahead of her. The streets were practically deserted and she quickened her pace to catch up with them. As Wesley opened the door of his pickup for Jack to jump in, Yelisa slid in under the steering wheel and put her arm around Jack. Wesley hesitated for a second then slid in beside her. He started the motor and Yelisa breathed again.

Without looking at her, he asked, "Your place or mine?"

"Where is your place?"

"Filson's Motel, number six."

"Mine, then. You know where it is?"

Wesley shook his head.

"You know where MacKenzie Mercury is."

Wesley nodded.

"Head for the mine and I'll show you where to turn."

They drove in silence, up into the hills.

Yelisa pointed. "There, that cattle guard on the left."

Wesley made the turn and they wound up a long lane. All at once they left the barren hillsides for the forest. A house loomed ahead. As they drew nearer, it took shape; a darker mass against the trees. It was an enormous Victorian mansion, complete with wooden lace, porches, turrets, gables, and a dozen chimneys. Wesley was fascinated. He parked in front, under the porte-cochere, and held the pickup door open for Yelisa and Jack. Yelisa opened the front door to the house.

Wesley spoke to Jack. "Stay."

Jack looked at him reproachfully but obeyed, curling up under a porch swing.

Yelisa took pity on him. "Let him come in."

"No."

She bent to pat Jack. "Hard-hearted, isn't he?"

Jack wagged his tail but didn't get up. Yelisa flipped the light switch as they entered and Wesley caught a glimpse of white lace and heavy old mahogany furniture as Yelisa led the way past the double parlor separated by the wide central hall and up the broad, curving stairs. She opened a door and they went into her sitting room. Wesley saw hundreds of books on shelves on two sides of the room. An expensive and very good entertainment system occupied one wall and a fireplace took up most of the fourth. The room was decorated in pale green with ivory accents and was comfortably modern without doing too great violence to the integrity of the architecture.

Yelisa asked, "Do you want a drink?"

"No."

She led the way into her bedroom. She crossed to a table beside the king size bed and turned on a lamp that gave a soft, rosy glow to the room. This room was also done in pale green and ivory. She removed the cover from the bed and folded the bedclothes back. She turned to Wesley and stood in front of him uncertainly. He took her in his arms and kissed her gently.

He whispered against her hair. "Getting undressed is always the awkward part."

"Do it for me."

Wesley unsnapped her shirt and slipped it off. He fumbled with her bra until she reached back and unhooked it, letting it fall. She sat on the chaise longue and he knelt to pull off her boots and socks. He rose and scooped her up, nuzzling his face against hers, letting his mouth move over her neck and shoulders. He carried her to the bed and put her gently down. He unbuckled her belt, unbuttoned her jeans, unzipped them and slowly pulled them off.

He stood watching her for a moment, thinking how lovely she looked with her hair fanned out on the pillow and her skin glowing in the rosy light. Still watching her, he unsnapped his shirt and quickly undressed. He slid onto the bed beside her and she buried her face in the curve of his neck. Wesley held her close, then tipped her head back and kissed her lips. He was piqued. Her love-making was new to him; very unlike those women he'd been used to who prized a satisfactory performance above romance and tenderness. No, it wasn't new; memory stirred. Back in his youth there had been girls like this. Shy and uncertain. It had been a long time ago. It was exciting now, to hold her and move against her body while she clung to him, her uneven breath on his neck.

Later, as they were lying on their backs with Yelisa cradled in Wesley's arms, he held her to him and there was an astonished tenderness in his face as he looked at her. There hadn't been any skyrockets and the earth hadn't quaked but Yelisa was quite happy. Wesley's reaction had revealed the extent of the power she held and she was reveling in the knowledge that she could make this strong man tremble and whisper his surrender.

Suddenly, Wesley sat up, looking down at her with panic-stricken eyes. Yelisa was obviously not a woman of great sexual experience and an awful thought had just occurred to him.

"You do practice birth control, don't you?" he asked, doubting that she did.

Yelisa shook her head unconcernedly. "No. I haven't had any reason to."

"Of course not," he said and looked so dismayed that Yelisa laughed.

He stared at her and she laughed harder.

"It's not funny," he told her indignantly. "Damn. What are you laughing at?"

Yelisa pulled him down to her. "What difference does it make? We'll make a baby sooner or later, why not the very first time?"

"I don't make babies."

Yelisa nibbled his earlobe. "I think you will," she said softly.

Wesley looked into her eyes, searching for some clue to her real feelings. What he saw satisfied him that she wasn't playing some kind of game. She honestly believed what she said. He crushed his mouth against hers and she slid her arms under his to hold him tightly to her.

Wesley didn't sleep at all that night. Yelisa fell asleep with her head on his shoulder and he held her protectively, wondering at the incredible luck that had befallen him. Why should a woman like Yelisa love him? Would she continue to love him when she knew him better? Was it possible she could love an itinerant ranch hand? How about a reasonably successful musician? He'd given up all hope of happiness twenty years ago but he hadn't been unhappy in the intervening years. There were highlights to look back on and savor. Now here was happiness thrusting itself toward him again. Was it obtainable? Could he and Yelisa really be happy together? These questions plagued him until he looked at his sleeping lady. Then everything seemed simple and easy. They would be married and live happily ever after. Nonsense. Nobody lived happily ever after. The room cooled and he pulled the sheet up to cover them. When a blanket became necessary, he tucked it around Yelisa. The dew would be falling, it was time to bale hay.

Yelisa stirred as he moved toward the edge of the bed and she reached for him. He kissed her eyelids and her mouth. She moved closer to him, not opening her eyes, and caressed his face and neck.

He spoke quietly. "The dew is falling, Yelisa. And Mr. Radzinski pays me to bale hay when the dew is falling. I've got to go."

Yelisa replied dreamily. "If you gotta go, go now, or else you got to say all night."

"Go back to sleep."

Yelisa opened her eyes and sat up. "When will I see you again?"

Wesley got out of bed and headed for the bathroom, gathering up his clothes on the way. "Tonight. Wear your prettiest dress and I'll meet you at Dightman's for dinner."

Yelisa smiled at him and snuggled down under her blanket, asleep almost before he closed the bathroom door.

Wesley stopped for a glass of milk on his way out to the pickup. As he was putting the carton away, a slight rustling sound caused him to turn around. He was startled to see a tiny middle-aged woman, wearing a quilted satin robe of bright blue, holding a double-barreled, twenty-gauge shotgun pointed at his middle. He stared at her for a moment then relaxed against the counter and sipped his milk.

The woman was Agnes Pratt, Yelisa's housekeeper, cook, and honorary aunt. Agnes was devoted to her as only a woman who's lived all her life for other people, only to have them grow up or die and leave her unneeded, can be devoted when someone declares a new need for her. Yelisa's need had been very great when her parents were killed and Agnes had filled the void as well as might be.

She spoke steadily and sternly. "What are you doing in my kitchen?"

Wesley gestured with his glass. "Drinking my breakfast."

"Smart guy. Who are you?"

"Wesley Callaghan."

Agnes was suspicious. "I have a CD by a man named Wesley Callaghan. And I heard he was singing at the Pastime. Would that be you?"

"Yes, ma'am."

Agnes peered closely and allowed the shotgun muzzle to drop. "I don't believe a word of it. Callaghan was killed in a car wreck or something. Plane crash, maybe."

"What makes you think he's dead?"

Agnes snorted. "A man that can sing and play like that? A man with more fans than can fill the stadiums? A man with a million women at his feet? He's going to make just one record?"

"I did, though." He finished the milk. "Listen, it's been real nice talking to you, but Mr. Radzinski pays me to bale hay and I have to get to work."

Wesley politely rinsed the glass at the sink. As he went out the kitchen door to the hall, Agnes raised the muzzle of the shotgun and followed.

"If you don't have anything on tonight," Wesley said, "drop in at the Pastime. I have a hunch I'll be playing there."

He went down the hall and outside. He opened the pickup door and pulled a fringed buckskin jacket out. He put it on while Jack jumped in and stood on the seat licking his face.

Agnes watched and said, "I don't believe a word of it."

When Wesley had driven away, Agnes leaned the shotgun against the wall and hurried up the stairs. She knocked perfunctorily on Yelisa's door and flung it open. Yelisa propped herself up on one elbow to look at Agnes.

"There was a man downstairs just now," Agnes told her, "said his name was Wesley Callaghan. Acted just like he owned the place."

"He does," Yelisa said, and smiled.

"I always said when you fell for a man, you'd fall hard. I hope you're not going to regret it. A man that good-looking isn't to be depended on."

"Wesley will want his breakfast tomorrow morning about four-thirty. Is that too early for you?"

"Art went to work in the woods at five o'clock, five days a week for twenty-three years. Breakfast was always at four-thirty. It might be nice to have someone to cook for again."

Wesley drove into an alfalfa field where the windrows were raked and turned, ready for baling. He took a can of dog food, a can opener, and a dish out of the space behind the driver's seat. He fed Jack, patting him fondly. Then he walked over to the baler, checked to make sure it had wire and that the tractor had oil and gas, started it up and moved it into position on the windrow. The sun was making deep red streaks in the sky. The baler made a monotonous clackety-clackety sound as Wesley followed the windrow round and round. When it got too warm to bale, he stopped the machine and walked back to the pickup, whistling for Jack. The dog came running from a rock pile where he'd been hunting rock squirrels and Wesley hunkered down to play with him a minute.

He stopped at the cottage to check its condition and was glad to find that Trudy had left it clean. It seemed a long time ago that he and Trudy had shared the cottage. When Wesley drove into the ranch headquarters, Burt Radzinski was crossing his yard from the house to the shop.

They stood in the shade of the building and Wesley reported his progress on the alfalfa field. Radzinski nodded and then stared as Wesley added that he'd like to draw his time.

"You're quitting?" Radzinski asked in surprise.

"Yes, sir. I'm sorry to leave you in the middle of haying and I'll stay until you get someone else, but only a day or two."

"You're a top hand, Callaghan. If you've had a better offer, I can sweeten your check a little."

"Well, sir, I've had a better offer, but I don't think you can top it. It's a whole other kind of work."

"All right. I'll go to town and see what I can find."

"I've moved out of your house." Wesley took the key out of his pocket and handed it over. "I drove by just now and it's all cleaned and ready for your new hand."

"Thanks, the missis'll appreciate that."

"I'll finish baling that field and start raking the upper one as soon as the dew falls again. But I'll be taking the rest of today off."

"All right," Radzinski shrugged.

Chapter 5

Wesley had made his decision. He would work with Monte and the boys for a few weeks, maybe for the rest of their itinerary. If it was okay, if people still liked him, and if he liked performing, he'd think about a comeback. If it didn't work out, he could write. He knew he'd barely tapped his song-writing talent. Or maybe he'd buy a ranch and turn gentleman farmer. He'd think of something, if he could convince Yelisa to marry him. He was nearly frantic all at once. He wanted Yelisa beside him. A home to come back to. His work. The work he was fitted to do and that he loved. He saw it all before him and was terrified it would slip away before he could grasp it.

Money. That was the first thing he'd better attend to. He'd given most of his ready cash to Trudy. There was a lot of money lying around in his name somewhere. The fruits of his early singing career. He'd given his father, who was a businessman in Los Angeles, the handling of it and he'd only occasionally drawn on it. It had given him pleasure to live on what he made as a ranch hand. Now it was different. He'd need clothes, traveling money, and there were things he wanted to buy for Yelisa. A ring, for openers.

Wesley went into a phone booth and called his father at his office. He explained the situation and asked his dad to wire a substantial sum to the Fossil bank. Brad Callaghan was amazed and a little apprehensive. Wesley wanting to get married? He'd never thought to hear that news. It took him a while to assimilate everything Wesley was saying. But he was behind his eldest all the way. Yes, he'd sit tight and wait for a call from the bank.

When Wesley had rung off, Brad did a computer check for Fossil, Oregon and found it was the county seat of Wheeler County, population 960. A little calculation and he found that the county as a whole had 1550 people, a population density of nearly one person per square mile. A quick survey of the surrounding counties and he concluded that Wesley had landed in the back of beyond. He couldn't imagine how or why his eldest son came to be there but maybe it was going to be a good thing. He'd never understood Wesley but he respected him. Brad Callaghan called his wife and she asked a lot of questions that he couldn't answer. But she shared his hope that Wesley was going to be happy.

Wesley went into the bank and spoke to the teller, a pretty young woman who referred him to an officer behind the railing. The bank officer was a sour-faced old guy who'd been turning cowboys down for auto loans for so many years that he automatically scowled when he saw a cowboy enter the building. Since Wheeler County contained few men who didn't at least dress like cowboys, the scowl was more or less permanent.

Wesley explained the situation concerning his bank wire and opened an account so there would be a place to put the money.

The bank officer called Wesley's father and gave him the account number. Brad Callaghan would go immediately to his own bank and complete the transaction. Wesley asked for the phone and thanked his dad. The bank officer looked a little dazed as Wesley hung up the phone and left.

Wesley's next stop was the Fossil Drug and Variety Store. Then he went into Warner's General Mercantile and bought a blue western shirt. At Isbister's General Store he bought a new hat with a fancy hatband.

Then he went to Dightman's to have a talk with Monte. They sat in the little kitchen-living room drinking beer, discussing the possibilities.

"How do the other guys feel about it?" Wesley asked. "Did you talk it over with them?"

"They couldn't be happier, Wes. I told 'em it was nothing definite yet, but I'd asked you to come back. Every one of 'em wants you to."

"I'm going to give it a try. How much longer are you going to be here?"

"Hot damn!" Monte grinned and crushed his empty beer can. "I could just hug and kiss you, boy."

"That'll be taken care of more appropriately. How long?"

Monte went to the refrigerator and got a fresh round of beers. "It's open. We were originally booked for two weeks but we got a hole in the itinerary and the management likes us. The next gig is a county fair down in Klamath Falls. That's in August."

"That gives us, what, three weeks here?"

"Two and a half."

"All right. We're working good together but we need rehearsal time. I've got to bale hay another couple of days. After that, my time's my own."

"What about publicity? Shall I call Robbie and tell her to put out a release?"

"I guess we'd better. We'll have to make a splash." Monte nodded and Wesley continued, "What do you want me to do, Monte? Guest shots for a while? Featured vocalist?"

"I'd like you to lead again."

"I can't do that. Not yet, anyway. This is what I thought: I can sing one or two numbers a set; or we can alternate sets."

They threshed it out from every angle until Monte had to get suited up for the show and Wesley went back to Filson's to shower and change into his new finery.

He was waiting at Dightman's when Yelisa came in. He'd taken a table in a dimly lit corner and Yelisa slipped into the chair next to his, smiling happily. He took her hand in both of his. She was dressed in her usual jeans and cowboy boots but instead of a shirt she wore a pale blue sweater. The waitress bustled up with menus and turned to leave.

Wesley stopped her. "Wait a minute. I think we know what we want."

Yelisa nodded.

The waitress took her pen and pad out of her pocket. "Cocktails first?"

Wesley looked the question at Yelisa. She shook her head.

"Not tonight," he said.

Yelisa ordered. "I'll have the New York, Mabel, medium well, baked potato, Italian dressing."

"Make it two," Wesley said, "but make mine medium rare. And hold the salad."

"And what to drink?" Mabel asked.

Wesley ordered milk and Yelisa asked for iced tea. Mabel hurried away.

"Are we in a hurry tonight?" Yelisa asked.

"Just to get rid of unnecessary interference." He turned her hand over and kissed the palm. "I quit my job today."

Yelisa laughed.

"Why's it funny?" he asked.

"Agnes will be so disappointed."

"Agnes is the little lady with the shotgun?"

"Shotgun?"

"Sure's you live and breathe. There I was drinking a glass of milk in your kitchen, just as peaceful and minding my own business. And in comes this little bit of a woman packing a twenty-gauge aimed right at my solar plexus."

"She didn't tell me about the twenty-gauge. I told her you'd be wanting breakfast at four-thirty every morning, though. She thinks it'll be nice to have someone to cook for."

"You don't count? Or doesn't she cook for you?"

Mabel served the salad and Yelisa thanked her.

"Oh, she cooks for me but I don't really count," she said. "She says it's not fun because I don't eat enough. Maybe I can do better after we get our baby started."

For just a moment, Wesley's heart was in his eyes. He gave a look of wistful longing then he reached into his pocket and tossed a small blue box out on the table. Yelisa took a bite of salad and picked up the box.

"I told you I don't make babies," he said flatly.

Yelisa picked up the box interestedly. "Condoms? I never say any before." She read the label. "'Trojan-Enz. With special receptacle end. Lubricated for greater sensitivity. Every condom is individually tested.' Tested? How do they test

61

them? I thought these were throw-away items."
She opened the box and began to read again.
"How to Use a Condom. One. Place the condom
on the...'"

Wesley interrupted her. "Don't bother to read
the instructions. I know how they're used."

"Yeah, I bet you do."

She eyed him specutively, then pulled a string
of three small blue packets out of the box and
detached one, tearing it open carefully. She
unrolled it and wiped her hands on her napkin.
Then she blew it up. She contemplated it a
moment, ignoring the other diners, who were
staring at her. She jabbed the condom with her
steak knife. It made a satisfying pop and part of it
flew across the room. Wesley and Yelisa
continued to ignore the other diners.

"All right," he said. "Here's the deal: I'll help
you make a baby if you'll marry me."

Yelisa was doubtful. "I don't know. It might
be fun to be married to you." She grinned at him.
"Entertaining as hell!"

"What's the problem, then?"

Mabel arrived with the steaks and her eyes
popped when she took the salad plate and saw the
remains of the condom. She looked at Wesley,
then at Yelisa, blushed scarlet and retired with the
salad plate. Yelisa called her back and she
returned reluctantly. Yelisa held up the condoms,
the wrapper, and the box.

"You might as well take these, too."

Mabel held out the plate and Yelisa dropped them onto it. The waitress hurried away.

Wesley repeated his question. "What's in the way of you marrying me?"

"I'm not sure whether you would understand why I would if I did. Is that coherent?"

"Barely."

"It's not the baby."

"I know."

"I mean, I wouldn't marry you or anybody just in order to have one. Or to legitimize one."

"I know."

"Oh, Wesley. Do you really? It's so hard to share your feelings and dreams with people without them making a hash of them. I'd almost given up when suddenly, there you were, across a crowded room, just like the song says. I thought maybe you'd be the one who could understand. The one who would understand. Take the trouble to know me and listen to me, I mean."

Wesley closed his eyes for a moment. "I really do know what you're looking for. I really do want to help you find it. If you find it, I think I'll have found it, too. You see, I'm very honest about my selfishness."

Yelisa smiled at him. "It's one of your most attractive traits."

"What does the baby mean to you?" he asked.

"Freedom from fear. You have to be very sure of yourself before you begin a new human life. You and I can help each other to that certainty. I guess the baby is a symbol of self-assertion. At least until it's an actual baby."

"I don't think statistics will bear you out, Yelisa."

"I know, I know. But I'm not talking about people in general. I'm talking about us."

"I've always been more afraid of fathering a child than of anything in the world."

"Why? Is it money? Because if that's all, I've got plenty. Mercury has a fairly steady demand."

"Money is not one of my hang-ups. We can use yours or mine. If we both run out, we'll earn some more."

"All right, Wesley, I'll marry you."

"Tomorrow."

"We can get the license tomorrow. But I'd like to wait until Sunday for the ceremony."

"That means a minister, I suppose."

"Do you mind having the minister?"

"It's okay if it doesn't include a promise from you to obey me. I can see that you have no intention of being an obedient wife."

"What tipped you off?"

"Look at you. I distinctly told you to wear your prettiest dress."

"I didn't feel like getting all gussied up in a dress."

"I love you."

"I love you," she answered.

The waitress came to clear their plates away. "Would you care for dessert?"

Wesley looked up at her. "Mabel, where's the nearest jewelry store?"

Mabel's eyebrows rose in surprise. "There's one in Condon."

"Thank you. Miss MacKenzie and I are engaged and I want to buy her a ring."

Mabel was really surprised. "Congratulations, Yelisa. I'm real happy for you both."

Yelisa glanced at her. "Thanks, Mabel. We don't care for dessert but we'll have a bottle of champagne."

Mabel went to fetch the wine.

They went from Dightman's to the Pastime where the management had reserved Yelisa's table without her phoning for it. When they arrived the band was playing an instrumental. Wesley held his hand out to Yelisa and they danced a courtly cheek-to-cheek. In the middle of the applause, the band broke into a raucous number that was one of Yelisa's favorites. They danced to the exciting beat and as the song ended, Wesley saw Agnes sitting at a table with a couple of her friends. They all had drinks and appeared to be enjoying themselves. Agnes waved and Wesley waved back. He took Yelisa back to the table and mounted the band platform.

Monte introduced him. "Mr. Wesley Callaghan, folks! Wes has been out of circulation for a few years but now he's back. Are you glad to see him?"

The applause was very enthusiastic as the crowd welcomed Wesley. He looked out at them solemnly, took the guitar Monte handed him and dropped his hand in a pre-arranged signal to the band. For the last song of the set he asked Yelisa to join him on the bandstand and when she was beside him, he spoke into the mike.

"Yelisa and I just got engaged, folks. Let's celebrate! Monte, would you use your drag with the management and ask him to chalk up the rest of the drinks tonight to my score? Is that okay, Mr. Clayton?"

Clayton was tending bar. "It's okay with me if Yelisa guarantees it."

Yelisa grinned at Clayton, "Hey, whatever Wesley says is okay with me."

The audience clapped and several people offered her advice but it was all good humored fun. The waitress and Clayton served a new round of drinks and Wesley asked Yelisa to sing for him. She told the band what she wanted and they began to play. After that she asked Wesley for a song that was very special to her, an old standard that everyone could relate to. When he finished, he handed the guitar back, raised his arms in his characteristic benediction, and left the stage with Yelisa. They went out of the Pastime arm-in-arm, the applause following them through the door.

They collected Jack outside and drove part of the way to Yelisa's. Wesley pointed out the moonrise and they stopped to watch it climb over the hills into the stars. Jack sat on the seat beside Yelisa, pawing at her for attention.

Wesley reprimanded him. "Down, Jack."

Jack put his head on his paws and looked at him reproachfully. Yelisa stroked his fur.

Wesley happened to touch Yelisa's belt and it reminded him that he meant to ask her about the trophy buckle. He fingered it, tracing the outline of the horse and rider.

"Where did you win your buckle? And for what?"

"I got lucky in the cutting-horse competition at Spray six or seven years ago."

"I thought the clothes and boots were mostly costume effect. Oh, Lord, I've done gone and fell in love with a real cowgirl."

"Cowgirls aren't for falling in love with?" she asked.

"How am I going to maintain any sort of macho image with a woman who's just as competent as I am?"

Yelisa pressed her body against his. "We could go home and work on your image now," she suggested.

Wesley kissed her and nestled his face against her neck. Jack gave his cheek a friendly swipe with his tongue and Wesley sat up and wiped his hand across his face.

"Damn dog," he said mildly. "Maybe we'd better go on home."

Yelisa was puzzled for a moment but deduced what must have happened and laughed. Wesley settled back with his arm comfortably around her.

"What kind of wedding do you really want?" she asked.

'Whatever kind it takes."

They sat watching the moon for some minutes.

Yelisa broke the silence. "My parents are both dead. My grandparents have all gone to their various rewards. I do have a sister. She's got three kids. I love the kids, like my brother-in-law – a little – and detest my sister. Do we have to invite them to our wedding?"

"Not if you'd rather not. I have parents, one brother, twin sisters, a passel of aunts, uncles, and cousins, and one grandmother. I adore them all. Except for a couple of cousins and one aunt – but I don't particularly want them at our wedding."

"It's just as well, since the bride can't wear white."

Wesley turned to face her squarely, surprised that she even knew the old shibboleth. "Would you rather wear white or spend the night with me?"

"Wear white. I can sleep with you anytime."

"You little devil."

Yelisa laughed softly and Wesley started the motor and backed around into the road.

She was very sure of herself the second night. She was blithe as she ran up the stairs and switched on the rose lamp. She folded the bedclothes back and had begun to unsnap her shirt when she turned and saw Wesley watching her intently. She became constrained in the face of his passion, forgetting herself in her desire to please him. Wesley saw the change come over her face and recognized the look.

When he was much younger, Gayle had looked at him like that and he hadn't had the experience to know it for the harbinger of failure that it was. He had accepted Gayle's gift and her assurance that she was satisfied. For her part, Gayle had assumed that in giving Wesley pleasure, she was fulfilling herself. Neither of them had realized that she was accumulating a store of resentment that she refused to acknowledge. So their love had been killed by a sacrifice that Wesley had neither recognized nor wanted and that had betrayed Gayle who had only wanted to please him.

He'd spent a lot of time and pain figuring out what went wrong between himself and Gayle. He was ready to try again with Yelisa but he wanted her as a partner, not some sort of burnt offering. He sat back in the chaise and pulled her onto his lap.

Later, as they lay in bed cuddled closely, their hair tousled and a little damp at the hairline, Yelisa couldn't remember at what point they had moved to the bed from the chaise. But she was conscious of feeling spent and happy and gloriously, contentedly sated.

She curled comfortably into his arm and reached up to trace the outline of his mouth. "I love the contrast – smooth lips and rough whiskers. And your hands."

She picked up his free hand and studied it. Turning it over, she kissed the palm and placed it on her breast.

Wesley was frightened. He was feeling that the gods don't care to see mortals too happy and that disaster of some sort would surely strike. His love for Yelisa burgeoned and his thoughts seethed and roiled. Self-doubt possessed him and made him a coward.

"Are you sure?" he asked. "You don't know much about me. You don't even know if I can earn a living. Maybe I'm marrying you for your money."

Yelisa smiled up at him. "I'll risk it."

Wesley cried out, "You don't know the risk! You don't know how badly I could hurt you."

'No. But you know. So you know how badly I can hurt you. You're willing to risk it. And you said yourself you're a selfish man – not that I believe it – ergo: I'm not in any danger of being badly hurt."

Wesley kissed her hair, reassured and at peace. Yeah, he knew the risk and he knew the pain. He hadn't suffered, really suffered, from a love affair for many years but the memory, though dimmed, wasn't erased. Yeah, he knew the pain that lovers can inflict on each other. But he also knew that Yelisa wouldn't use his love as a weapon against him. He sighed, as one released from a long, tense vigil, but all he said was, "Okay."

Yelisa hugged him and presently asked, "Why did you abandon your career?"

"Pain."

She was silent a long moment, thinking it over. "Like sending me away from Lava Flat? Because your need was so great you didn't want to run the risk of disappointment?"

"Yeah. Music has always been the motivating force in my life. When I cut those sides, I loved that music. I knew that the so-called serious critics didn't think much of it. But a lot of it was really good. And I also knew that the boys and I would grow and mature and our music would grow with us. Then I learned about reality. Other people controlled the recording equipment and the distribution machinery. Other people had to be consulted about our work. It frightened me. It scared me so bad that I quit rather than compromise anymore."

"I see."

Wesley was faintly surprised. "I believe you do see."

"I think so. It's kind of like being asked to assist with your own execution. You're going to die but you don't have to help the bastards kill you."

"Yeah. Yeah, that's how I felt. So I decided to do something as completely removed from the music business as possible."

There was laughter in her voice as she asked, "Bucking hay?"

"Bucking hay," he agreed. "I've missed the joke again."

"You can't keep from doing the creative, can you? You take the notes and string them together into your music. Or you take alfalfa and wire and make hay to sustain the livestock through the winter."

"And you're a miner. You dig the ore out, process it, and extract the mercury. Also a creative job. I never thought of it all in just this light before."

"Of course not, you've never had me to explain it before."

'Where are we going to live? If I decide to make a comeback – and if I succeed – well, Fossil's a long way from anywhere else. It'll mean recording sessions, tours, personal appearances, TV dates. And your mercury mine is not portable."

"I wish I could tell you how grateful I am that you haven't assumed that I would sell it or turn it over to someone else to run," she said passionately. "Because I'll tell you now, right up front, that I don't believe in sacrifices and I have no intention of sacrificing one single thing for you or anyone else."

"If only Diogenes could hear you. You must be the one honest person in the world."

"It was pretty bad sometimes?"

"Do you know that, too?" Wesley looked down into her eyes, wondering if this incredible woman could really understand how he felt. "Do you really understand? Tell me."

"I think," Yelisa said slowly, "that a lot of people tried to flatter you and use you. I don't mean in a fair trade where both parties receive value. I think you saw through the flattery, you have a pretty clear idea of your own worth, but I think it must have taken longer to see through the dishonesty. I think you were conned into believing that you owed people when the score was really even."

"How do you know all that?" Wesley demanded.

"Well, Fossil's a small town but people are much the same anywhere. My mother was a good teacher, too."

Wesley tightened his arm around her and she turned her face up to his kiss.

"I still don't see how we're going to manage to be together," he said.

"You must be very tired or something. We'll make our home here; build a new house if you don't like this one. We can have a second home in Hollywood or Nashville or Kona or wherever

73

you want it. Crosby used to commute from Elko, Nevada. And Elko's nearly as remote as Fossil."

"We can get a plane and learn to fly," Wesley said, with sudden inspiration. "Or hire a pilot. Whatever. Yelisa, you're wonderful."

"I think this is where I came in but I always like to see a really good show twice."

"You're going to see this one more than twice, lady."

He tipped her head back and his lips opened on hers.

Chapter 6

Agnes was at the stove cooking ham and eggs, fried potatoes and toast. Wesley was sitting at the table, sipping a glass of milk.

"Yelisa should be up to have breakfast with you," Agnes said.

"Why?" Wesley was one of the rare people of either sex who actually believed in human rights and had no wish to control anyone but himself.

"It's not right for a woman to send a man out to work while she stays in bed and sleeps."

"I don't see why not. She has her own work, her own schedule. And I like to think of her in bed."

Agnes disapproved of his attitude. She cared for Yelisa almost as much as she did for her own sons, but she had never approved of Yelisa's work or lifestyle. The girl ought to've got married years ago and let someone else take care of the business.

"When Art and I – Art was my husband. He passed away two years ago last month. We were married for thirty-two years. When we got married, I was proud to be his helpmate. Our home was run to suit his needs and we were very happy together. For thirty-two years. He died of cirrhosis of the liver."

Wesley felt a pang of sorrow for the waste. Thirty-two years of sacrifice for both man and wife. Neither of them had what they wanted but Agnes was still protecting the perfidious tenets of her life. He understood that she couldn't change her attitude without admitting that Art had been destroyed in her immolation.

"Did Yelisa tell you that we're going to be married?"

"She did. And a good thing, too. I don't hold with this new morality."

She dished up his breakfast and set the plate in front of him. He ate appreciatively, but not heartily, and she began to assemble a lunch for him. "I'll bet Art liked ham and eggs the way you cook 'em."

"He liked a well-cooked meal," she said complacently.

"Well, you surely haven't lost your touch, ma'am. This is the best breakfast I've had in a good long time."

If the way to a man's heart was through his stomach, the way to Agnes' heart was also through a man's stomach. She was highly gratified. "I'm glad you're enjoying it."

"Do you do all the housework?"

Agnes poured a cup of coffee. "Except for the spring and fall heavy cleaning. Rita Samuels generally helps with that. And Homer Cassidy does the yard and takes care of Yelisa's horse."

"I just want you to know that I appreciate the fine job you do. Clean sheets every night, fresh towels, everything dusted and shiny."

Agnes set the coffee in front of Wesley and spoke a little belligerently. "Yelisa's given you the rights of a husband in this house but she's more than a daughter to me. If you hurt that girl, I've still got the shotgun."

Wesley handed the coffee back to her. "I seldom drink coffee, ma'am. It's habit-forming and hard on the liver."

Agnes took the cup and put it on the counter, returning to the table with his lunch. He pushed his plate away.

"I think we understand each other," he said. "Don't we, Aggie? We'll both do what's best for Yelisa." He stood up and picked up his hat and lunch. "Let her sleep."

Before she knew what his intention was, he'd leaned down and kissed her cheek. He went down the hall. She stood with her hand on her cheek and watched him go.

"I don't believe a word of it," she declared.

Yelisa wore a natural-colored linen dress and low-wedge pumps as a concession to the importance of the occasion. She and Wesley planned to go over to Condon and pick out the ring after they got the license at the court house.

But she'd had to go to the office first and the day had not been going smoothly. It was one of those days when everyone was rushed and impatient. She had gone to the plant to talk over the second shift with the foreman and Tom Plank had been there and had come back to her office with her. She picked up her handbag from her desk.

"Did you check out the charges Merryman's using?" she asked.

"Not yet, I've…"

Yelisa interrupted. "Do it today. He's using more than he needs; he's going to blow himself up."

"Okay, I'll check it out. Listen, Yelisa, what about this Callaghan character?"

She looked at him with raised eyebrows. "What about Mr. Callaghan?"

"Well, you hardly know the man."

She spoke calmly and firmly. "You're a good mine superintendent, within certain limitations, and I'd be sorry to let you go. But you'd better stick to mining when you speak to me."

Tom, who saw all his careful preparation going for naught, tried to stay calm but his voice vibrated with the intensity of his feelings. "Will you listen a minute? For your own good? I was hoping I wouldn't have to tell you this. But I guess I'd better." Yelisa scowled at him but he continued doggedly on. "There's a girl here in town, she lives in one of those trailers Tony

Warren moved in last year. She's pregnant and she says it's Callaghan's baby."

Yelisa spoke icily. "Tom, I know you've been hoping that you could snare the boss lady and her money and I haven't paid much attention because you are good at your job. But you were never in the running as a husband and you aren't that good a superintendent. Don't you ever question anything in my private life again."

"But, Yelisa..."

She interrupted with one word that fell like a black frost in the room. "Tom." When she was sure he was squelched, she left the office and got into the Mercedes.

Yelisa thought about Tom and the office until she drove into her driveway. Wesley would be coming soon, she thought happily. She sat in one of the rattan chairs on the porch to wait for him. She was dreaming the dreams she'd been postponing for years when he drove in and parked behind her car. Jack ran to her and she petted him as she watched Wesley mount to the porch. She came forward to meet him and they kissed their greeting.

"You're looking very cool and regal today," he said as they went into the house and up the stairs. "I need a shower and about a quart of water."

Yelisa put her arm around his waist. "I need to talk to you about something."

Wesley kissed her ear. "Mm-hmm?"

She pushed him into an easy chair and crossed the sitting room to the concealed refrigerator. She filled a tall glass with ice and water.

Wesley was surprised. For the first time he really looked at the room, at the entertainment wall and discreet wet bar and comfortable furnishings.

"A real cozy setup. It might have been designed specially as a love nest."

Yelisa carried the glass to him and sat on his lap. He turned her so he could look into her eyes.

"It was," she said with a smile. "I always meant to take a lover when I had time."

"Far-sighted little wench, aren't you?"

"I try to think ahead."

Wesley drank about half the water and put the glass down. "I love you."

Yelisa's lips met his in a long kiss. She squirmed and arched her back to get closer to him.

"That's lovely," she whispered. "Do it again."

Wesley drank the rest of the water and kissed her again. Presently, she leaned back against his arm and he moved his other hand to cup her knee.

"You said we need to talk?" he asked.

It took Yelisa a moment to organize her thoughts and remember what it was she wanted to discuss. "There's a story going around that there's a girl living in town who's going to bear your child."

Wesley looked into her eyes. He couldn't tell whether he was under attack or not. He didn't think experience would help him because Yelisa's mind worked differently from anyone he'd ever known. He was afraid that his happiness was about to be wrecked but he had to be honest with this woman. "Do you believe it?"

"I don't think that's the point."

Not the point. That really confused him. He didn't believe he'd ever fathered a child but a couple of times paternity had been the point of some heavy conversations because someone had believed, or pretended to believe, that he had. "What is the point?"

"If it is your child, we'll take care of it. If it isn't, I'd like to stop the talk. It's a small town and I'd rather our neighbors thought well of us than not, if it isn't too much trouble."

Wesley was completely bewildered. Public opinion was the last thing he'd expected Yelisa to worry about. "Is blowing up and popping a condom in Dightman's dining room the best way to set about getting your neighbor's respect?"

She laughed. "I said if it isn't too much trouble."

He supposed he'd better tell her about Trudy. Surely, she was not naïve enough not to have known there would be Trudies in his past. He could wish not in such immediate past.

"Trudy came to Fossil with me. I've known her a total of about two-and-half months. She had no periods in the time she was with me and I took particular care not to impregnate her. The child is not mine. I gave her some money to go back to L.A. and I thought she had gone."

She nodded. "We'll give it some thought, how to deal with her."

That's all? Wesley was incredulous. No tears, no tantrums? Just a simple, practical attitude? "Do you believe me?" he asked again.

"Don't give me that power, Wesley," she said earnestly. "Don't let other people define your actions."

"Publish and be damned?"

"Yes. If you do what's right, don't let anyone stampede you into believing it's wrong. If you do what's wrong, correct it if you can. But never submit to blackmail – emotional or any other kind."

Wesley looked out over her head at something she couldn't see. He looked for what seemed like a long time. When he spoke, he astonished her. "I wish we'd met when we were kids. I've never had love like this."

"Neither have I," she answered.

Wesley gathered her in his arms and rose to carry her into the bedroom. He put her on the bed and kissed her.

Yelisa liked to drive and she enjoyed the way the Mercedes handled on the curvy road to Condon. She took the curves fast and was pleased to see that Wesley sat relaxed, didn't try to brake and never flinched. Wesley didn't exactly enjoy the drive; he'd much rather have done the driving himself. But, after all, it was her car and she was a good driver. Although it was only long familiarity with the road that allowed her to use that much speed. On a strange mountain, she'd have had to slow down.

There was only one jewelry store in Condon and it had only a few rings of the size and quality Wesley was interested in. He quickly eliminated all but a dozen or so. Some of the diamonds were good enough and there were a few emeralds he liked and one or two rubies. The sapphires he rejected because he disliked all sapphires. He took a long time making his selections while Yelisa watched indulgently. She didn't really care what color the stone was, except she'd rather have an emerald than a ruby. The clerk, who was also the owner, could hardly believe his good fortune. As a general rule he only sold rings in this price range after an exceptionally good harvest, usually at Christmastime. The customer didn't look like he had that kind of money but he was knowledgeable about the stones and he was buying it for Yelisa MacKenzie. So it must be all right.

Wesley set the rings he'd selected in a row on the black velvet tray and pushed it in front of Yelisa.

"Which one?" he asked.

Yelisa shook her head. "Whichever you like."

"No, you choose. These are all good stones, warranted to last as long as we do."

He held up a full carat pear-cut diamond. Yelisa shook her head. She picked them all up in turn and found that the more she looked at them, the more her preference for emeralds was confirmed. She finally tried on a big, square-cut emerald. It was lovely and the ring fit, she wouldn't have to wait while it was sized. Wesley nodded. She took it to the window to see how it looked in the sunlight. Wesley stood behind her. They looked from the emerald into each other's eyes and both were satisfied with what they saw.

They decided on plain gold for the wedding ring and Wesley chose a heavy, thick band.

"Will you wear a wedding ring?" Yelisa asked him as he was writing out the check.

He looked up at her. "I was beginning to wonder if I was going to be left out."

The clerk took Wesley's check, stamped it and put it in the till. Then he took out all the men's rings that could possibly be used for wedding rings. Yelisa set aside four carved gold rings, one with three small but good emeralds in a row, and two that matched her own plain gold circle.

"Which one?" she asked.

Wesley unhesitatingly picked up one of the plain ones. It was too big but the other one fit. Yelisa smiled at him and wrote out her own check.

On the way out to the car, Yelisa gave him the keys and went around to the passenger's door. He stopped at a grocery store on the way out of town and picked up a couple of wine spritzers. There was only one place between Condon and home to stop so he pulled in at Dyer Park and they sat on a picnic table in the shade of a small grove of trees and drank. They talked very little, enjoying the moment of peace and contentment in the quiet of the trees. At last Wesley looked at his watch and remarked that the court house would be closing soon.

The Wheeler County Court House was a two-story brick structure with a daylight basement, an octagonal tower rising another story on one corner and a square tower rising another two stories on another corner. It was the nearest thing to a skyscraper in the county. There was only one other person on the walk as Wesley and Yelisa came out and went to the car, the marriage license in Wesley's pocket. He handed her the car keys as they walked, remarking that she could drop him at his rehearsal on her way to the office.

Once inside the car, they sat quite motionless, looking into one another's eyes. Wesley picked up Yelisa's hand and kissed the palm. She kissed his earlobe.

"What time is your rehearsal?"

"Rehearsal at three, show at eight."

Yelisa turned her hand to admire the way the emerald caught the light. "It's beautiful. I love you," she said.

"I know."

She grinned at him and he added, "I told Monte that he'd helped make me irresistible to you."

"How did he do that?"

"He told you I'm bad news to women. Women can't seem to resist what they think is a real bad hombre."

"There's some truth to that." She looked at him speculatively. "Is that what I want you for, to reform you? You know, I believe, in a way, it is. I want you to see yourself as I do. You really are a class act."

"Not if I don't get to rehearsal on time."

"Where is it?" she asked, switching on the ignition.

"According to Monte, it's the first building on the right as you enter the fairgrounds on the paved road."

Chapter 7

It was late afternoon a couple of days later when Wesley returned from town with a big suitcase and a couple of guitar cases. He left the guitars in the hall and took the suitcase upstairs. His mother had sent several of his fancy western costume shirts, a couple of pairs of handsome cowboy boots and his five gold records. He had asked for the shirts and boots because western clothes never went out of style, but the records were a surprise. He laid them on the floor in the order he'd earned them and sat on the end of the chaise and looked at them, old memories flooding his mind. He looked at them a long time before he gathered them up and put them on the dresser. Then he sat on the bed and phoned his mother.

"Wesley! Did you get everything all right?"

"Yeah. That's why I calling, to thank you."

"Do the shirts still fit all right?"

"Yeah. Everything's fine. Thanks for throwing in the records."

"Oh." She paused a moment. "I didn't know if I should. But then I thought, if you're going to be married and live there, you ought to have them in your home."

"It's okay, Ma. I'm glad you sent them. But Yelisa's already impressed. She doesn't need gold records to tell her how important I am."

"Wesley." She relented and laughed. "Okay, you always seem to see through me. I just wanted her to know..." She left the thought unfinished.

"Know what? That I wasn't always a bum?"

"Wesley." There was real distress in his mother's voice.

"It's all right, Ma. I know how disappointed you were when I quit singing. I'm glad you sent the records. They brought back a lot of memories."

"Well, good. When are we going to get a chance to meet her?"

"I don't know. The wedding's going to be Sunday. After the tour, maybe. I'm sorry."

"It's all right. I'd like to see you married, of course, but you have to do what's best for yourselves. Maybe you can come here for a visit after a bit."

"Maybe. I'll be on the road for the next few weeks."

Donna Callaghan laughed. "Some honeymoon for the poor girl; dragged all over the country on a tour."

"She's not coming with us, Ma."

"Wesley!"

"I love the way you say my name when you're scandalized. It's okay, Yelisa understands. She agrees."

"I feel sorry for her already."

"No need. She's an extremely lucky girl. She's getting me and five gold records. What more could a girl ask? Listen, Ma, I've got to go now. You take care of yourself and I'll be in touch. Thanks for sending the stuff."

"You're welcome. Bye, Wesley."

"Bye, Ma."

Jack was sitting on the porch watching for him when Wesley went outside. He took one of his guitars out with him and sat down on the step next to Jack and played with the dog for few minutes. Something in the yard attracted Jack's attention and he trotted off to investigate. Wesley took the guitar out of its case and started to play, running over the same phrase again and again. Jack returned, sitting alertly at Wesley's feet, watching his face. Wesley stopped playing to stroke him.

Wesley was back at work on his music, playing different bits, when Yelisa drove in. She was wearing a tailored navy skirted suit, her hair was twisted into a knot and she looked every inch the lady executive. She sat on the steps with her arm around Jack, smiling up at Wesley. He put the guitar down and shooed Jack out of the way, moved up a step and began to massage her shoulders. She took her jacket off and sighed deeply. Wesley took the pins out of her hair and smoothed the heavy coil to its full length.

"You're a very useful person to have around," Yelisa said. "It's been a hard day and it isn't over yet. I have to go back after dinner."

"I thought maybe you'd been playing the heavy boss from that suit. It's very intimidating."

"It's supposed to be."

Wesley massaged her shoulders and neck in silence for a few moments.

'Wesley?"

"Mmmmm?"

"Would you like to see the mine and the plant?"

"I was waiting for an invitation."

"Why?"

"I didn't know whether it would be helpful to have me underfoot out there."

"I see. Can you come tomorrow? I'd like to show it to you."

Wesley moved down to sit beside her and took her hand. "What time?"

"About eleven-thirty?"

"All right."

They sat in companionable silence for a while.

"Oh, I nearly forgot," Wesley said. He reached in his pocket and pulled out a piece of paper and handed it to her. "I'm practicing. Good husbands always bring their paychecks straight home to their wives without stopping for even a single beer, I believe."

Yelisa laughed but didn't look at the check.

"Now, don't be making fun of my wages, woman. That represents the sweat of my brow."

She read the amount. "You've been working for this all these years?"

"Not all of 'em. I tried a lot of different things. I rode the rodeo circuit for two years. I'd have come out well up in the money, too, except old Prairie Schooner broke my leg and three ribs at Salinas."

"Bareback or saddle bronc?"

"Saddle bronc. I ain't crazy."

"Where did you win the buckle?"

"The All Indian in Fallon."

"How did you manage to enter? With you not being an Indian, I mean."

"Well, I was something of a rounder in those days. I was playing with this little combo in one of the bars in Fallon when the rodeo come on. I got to talkin' to one of the Indians – it was funny, he come up and laid a hundred dollar bill on the piano and said we could have it if we'd sing 'Rye Whiskey' for him. But we none of us knew the song. Anyway, one thing led to another and first thing I knew, I'd agreed to sign up for the saddle bronc ridin'. I can't remember the Indian's name. He was from Warm Springs, too. Well, the upshot was, he fixed it so's I could enter and I won the buckle. We stayed up all night doin' hoop dances and owl dances and I don't know what all."

Yelisa turned so she was lying across his lap and smiled up at him, patting his cheek. He bent his head to kiss her, cuddling her close.

"You've had a lot of fun, haven't you?" she asked.

"Off and on. Yeah, rodeoin' was fun. This is better."

Yelisa rose with sudden energy. "I want to get out of this rig and you've got to suit up. Let's go get undressed and see what develops."

"It's been developing ever since you drove in."

"I know."

Wesley was dressed for the stage, standing at the bedroom window, looking out into the driveway. Yelisa was sitting at her dressing table, putting the finishing touches on her eye makeup. She heard the sound of an approaching car.

"Who do we know drives a brown SUV?" Wesley asked.

"My sister's favorite color is brown. Is it new or old?"

"Newish."

Yelisa could hear the faint sound of voices and car doors opening and closing. Jack gave a couple of half-hearted barks.

Wesley continued his commentary. "It's a woman with two, no, with three kids. She doesn't look very happy."

Yelisa joined him at the window. She looked down and sighed. "Yes, that's Helen."

She looked at Wesley and grimaced. He looked back, wishing he could fend this nuisance of a sister from her but knowing there was not much he could do. He put his arm around her as they heard the front door slam.

Yelisa said, "I guess we'd better go down and get it over with. You're simply going to detest Helen."

"Maybe I'd better go on into town. I'll grab a bite to eat before the show. And you two girls can have your heart-to-heart talk privately."

She put her head on his shoulder. "I wonder who told her and what they said."

Wesley held her close for a moment, then led her out of the room and down the stairs.

Dinner wasn't as bad as he'd expected from Yelisa's gloom, but it wasn't a festive meal, either. Stuart was four, Allen was two-and-a-half, and Mary was just a year old. They were reasonably well behaved but a little mess was made. Helen was several years older than Yelisa and she tried very hard to be a trendy young pace-setter. She was feeding the baby rather impatiently. Yelisa wasn't bothering to hide her irritation that Helen had come and Wesley was wishing he had gone into town for dinner. Yelisa was right, he simply detested Helen. She sure expected a lot from the older boy.

As if to confirm his opinion, Helen spoke sharply. "Stuart, take the Jell-O away from Allen. Can't you see he's just messing in it?" She turned to Yelisa. "So you're going to get married at last? It reminds me of the old rhyme Grandma Lindow used to say – there never was a goose so gray but soon or late some gander took her for his mate."

Yelisa ignored the entire speech. "How's Stuart senior?"

Helen answered querulously. "I don't know what's the matter with him. Just because my income is larger than his, he seems to be getting more and more depressed. Of course, it's a lot larger, four or five times larger, but I always tell him it doesn't matter. As long as we love each other, it doesn't matter who has the money. Don't you agree, Wesley?"

He knew he shouldn't have done it, it didn't help Yelisa any, but his sense of humor couldn't resist it. "I certainly do. Why, I said to Yelisa just a night or two ago, I think it was the night before we got engaged, money is not one of my hangups, I told her. We can use yours or mine, either one. Isn't that what I said, Yelisa/"

"That's what you said," she confirmed, and murmured, "you rat."

Helen was displeased. "What do you do for a living, Wesley? Allen! Stop that! Do you want to be sent from the table? Straighten up and behave yourself." Allen stopped finger-painting in his mashed potatoes and Helen smiled at Wesley.

"Oh," Wesley said airily, "a little of this, a little of that. Bronc bustin', ranch handin'. Sometimes I pick up a little change singing in some bar."

Helen eyed him distastefully. "I see."

Wesley looked back at Helen. "I'm appearin' at the Pastime tonight and I don't want to be late. I want to give the people their money's worth. That's one of my principles – always give people their money's worth."

Yelisa spoke a little dryly. "It's too bad you have to go now. I'd just purely love to keep this little old conversation goin', but I know how it is. I'll walk you to the door."

Wesley jumped up and kissed her soundly before she could rise. "No, no. You just sit here and visit with your sister. I know my way to the door by now. I'll be home about two so don't y'all bother to wait up for me."

Yelisa glared after him as he hurried out the door and Helen's eyes were narrowed as she watched him go. The baby was yelling lustily, indignant at having been forgotten in the middle of her meal.

Helen spooned a bite to her and spoke to Yelisa. "Well, he's gorgeous, Yelisa. I'll give you credit for good taste as far as looks go. But it's perfectly obvious that he's marrying you for your money."

"If he is and it doesn't bother me, why should it bother you?"

Helen's mouth dropped open. "You know that's it?"

"No, of course it isn't. It's not my fantastic sexual prowess, either. He loves me for my mind."

"And why do you love him?"

"For his fantastic sexual prowess."

Helen scowled. "Would you please remember that my children are present? And try to be serious?"

"I love your children madly, Helen," Yelisa said with a grin, "and it's impossible to forget them. Especially when they're present." She turned to the boys. "Why don't you find Homer and get him to give you a ride on Firefly?"

Stuart climbed joyously down and Allen followed him.

Yelisa stopped them as they started for the kitchen door. "Wait a minute. What's the first thing you're going to do?"

"Ride the horse!" Stuart cried.

"Horsey! Horsey!" Allen agreed.

Yelisa shook her head. "No."

Stuart was very disappointed is Aunt Yelisa. "But you said."

Yelisa smiled at him. "The first thing is to find Homer. Okay?"

Stuart shouted okay and went through the swinging door into the kitchen. Yelisa listened to be sure Homer was there. Allen continued to shout horsey.

Yes, Homer was there. She heard him say, "Well, boys. When did you get here?"

"Today," Stuart answered. Aunt Yelisa says we can ride Firefly. After we find you."

"Looks like you found me. Let's get going while there's still daylight."

Allen was still yelling horsey as they clattered out the back door. Yelisa went into the hall bathroom and came back with a damp washcloth which she handed to Helen. As Helen washed Mary's hands and face, the baby protested and cried. Yelisa picked her up and took the cloth from Helen to finish. Mary squirmed and continued to protest until Yelisa put the cloth down. Helen lit a cigarette.

"If you're going to smoke, let's go out on the porch."

"Whatever."

As they went through the hall, Yelisa picked up a string of plastic disks from the top of the diaper bag. Helen sat in a rattan chair while Yelisa sat on the swing with Mary on her lap. Mary played with the disks, putting them in her mouth and waving them around while Yelisa dodged them.

"You'd better go ahead and say whatever you came to say," Yelisa told her sister. "I've got to go back to the office in a few minutes."

"Ruth Fischer called me day before yesterday and said it's all over town that you're shacked up with some cowboy, some cheap ranch hand. I didn't believe it at first but after she told me a few things, I thought I'd better come see for myself. And it's even worse than Ruth said."

Yelisa found Helen's drama half amusing, half exasperating. "How bad is it?"

"It seems he's dumped his wife or girlfriend to move in with you. And she's going to have a baby."

"Well, Helen, I'll tell you. Not because you have any right to ask, but because I know you won't leave me alone until I do. The woman is not Wesley's wife and the baby isn't his. I've always had a weakness for cowboys and Wesley and I are going to be married on Sunday."

"You are just plain crazy. Don't you know that you're pulling us all down to his level? Don't you see how he's degrading you?"

"That's enough," Yelisa said with ominous calm.

"No, it's not enough. Someone's got to make you see how impossible this whole thing is."

"It's not only possible, it's very nearly accomplished."

"I suppose you're going to let him run MacKenzie Mercury, too? You'll probably make him a gift of your stock."

Yelisa saw a great light and was surprised that she hadn't seen it sooner. So that was what Helen was worried about – her share of the profits. She laughed shortly. "My dear sister, no one is going to run MacKenzie Mercury but me.

Wesley has his own career; he's not interested in taking over mine. So you needn't worry about your dividend checks."

"That's what you think now. But mark my words, it'll be different after you're married."

Yelisa had no intention of discussing her marriage with Helen. She changed the subject abruptly. "How long are you going to stay?"

"I don't know. I didn't bring anything suitable to wear to a wedding. If there's really going to be one. I suppose I'd better go back to Bend and come back here Saturday."

Here was something to be nipped in the bud. And no time for tact, either. "I'm sorry if I gave you the wrong impression, but you are not invited to our wedding."

"Well, I didn't suppose you'd have the nerve to get yourself all decked out in white satin with the man living right here in the house with you, but I didn't think you were actually ashamed of him."

"Don't push it, Helen. Reverend Allison is going to perform the ceremony after church on Sunday. Mrs. Allison and Agnes will be the witnesses. You'll have to excuse me now. I have work to do."

Yelisa kissed Mary and put her on Helen's lap.

Chapter 8

Yelisa hadn't left any lights on, but the moonlight was bright and Wesley didn't have any problem finding his way through the quiet house. Yelisa was asleep on her stomach and Wesley stood beside the bed and let the love he felt for her well up and race through his body. He was still incredulous at the luck which had brought her to him. He undressed and slid into bed beside her. She turned to him, holding out one hand. He held it to his heart.

She said his name, sleepily and happily.

"Go back to sleep," he said softly.

She woke a little more. "How'd it go?"

"Good. It's going to be good. We're going to make it. Did your work go okay?"

Yelisa sat up, her bare shoulders gleaming in the moonlight. She was fully awake now. "The work was fine; mostly routine anyway. But Helen!"

"They're cute kids."

"You should see their father. He's the original Milquetoast. I think he and Helen married each other to see how unhappy one couple could make themselves."

"How long is she going to stay?"

"I hope she's going tomorrow."

"I suppose you heard all about my worthlessness," he said ruefully. "And Trudy."

"Did I ever. We ought to do something about Trudy, though."

"Why? I never made her any promises."

"I know. It's not really your responsibility. But...Queen Elizabeth the First said it. I can't quote her exact words but it's something like this: It is not the truth that is important, but what men believe to be the truth."

"I thought you said publish and be damned."

"I know. I guess I feel sorry for her. You were hers until I set my cap for you."

"I never was hers. We meant nothing to each other. She latched onto me because she needed a meal ticket. I let because I wanted a decoration for my bed."

"May I go to see her tomorrow?"

"Why?" Wesley was puzzled. "I don't think it's to check up on my story."

"No. But I want to find out what kind of woman she is, why she's staying on here instead of going back to her people in L.A. She's doing a lot of talking and I'd like to know why."

"You don't need my permission to see her."

"I wasn't exactly asking your permission. I think I was asking if you would mind. Because you're right, I do intend to see her."

"I don't mind. I gather you don't want me to go with you."

"You gather correctly."

She lay back down beside him and put her hand over his heart. There was a silence between them that changed from being merely the end of a conversation to being the beginning of something else.

"Your heart's starting to beat fast again," Yelisa whispered.

"How's my respiration?"

"A bit faster than normal. I think your temperature is rising, too."

"Is it contagious?"

"Very."

He put his hand over her heart. "You've got it, too," he said.

Yelisa went to the office early and when Wesley rose about ten, Agnes told him Helen and the children were out by the pool. He changed into a bathing suit and joined them, throwing his towel down on a chair. Helen was wearing white shorts and a hot pink tank top and was reclining in a chaise reading a magazine. She gave him a brief good morning and turned back to her story. Wesley joined the children.

Mary was sitting on the top step, splashing; Allen was hanging on the edge, kicking; Stuart was standing in water up to his chest watching

Wesley. Wesley eased into the water so an not to inundate the children.

"Can you float?" he asked Stuart.

"Sure. Watch."

Stuart put his arms out flat in front of him and did quite a creditable face float.

"That's pretty good," Wesley said when Stuart stood up. "How about doing a back float?"

"We only just learned face float," Stuart explained, shaking his head.

"I'll teach you how to back float, if you want."

Stuart grinned happily. "Oh, boy! Then I'd be ahead of Bobby Keller."

"Okay. First thing is to lay back in the water. I'll put my hand under you until you're ready for me to let go."

Stuart threw himself backwards in the water and Wesley just caught him before he got a face full of water and scared himself. He held the boy with one hand under the small of his back and straightened his arms and legs with the other.

"Are you ready? I'm going to let go now."

Stuart started to fold in half and Wesley put his hand back. After a couple more tries, Stuart was back floating all by himself. He went to tell his mother about it and Allen stood on the edge and hollered at Wesley.

"Me!"

'You want to float, too?"

"Yeah, I float."

Wesley towed him out away from the edge and repeated the lesson that Stuart had just finished. It took a little longer, but Allen caught on. While they were working, Mary left the step and wandered along the pool edge. Wesley saw her and parked Allen on the edge so he could fetch her back. Before he could get to her, she shrieked something unintelligible and jumped into the water. When she came up, Wesley was there to get her. He took her to the edge and stood her up.

"You want lessons, too?"

Mary patted his face, talking in her own jargon. Stuart and Allen came down the steps to practice back floating in the shallows. Wesley kept a sharp eye on them, especially Allen. He backed a couple of steps away from the edge and held his arms out to Mary.

"Okay, sweetheart, jump!"

Mary closed her eyes tightly and launched herself at Wesley, her arms outstretched. Wesley caught her and towed her toward the boys while he blew bubbles in the water. Mary put her mouth in the water and blew bubbles, too.

"That's right," Wesley told her. "Good."

He blew more bubbles and the boys noticed what he and Mary were doing. They began to blow bubbles. Wesley sat on the steps with Mary on his knee and the boys came to stand beside him.

"Can you dive?" Stuart asked.

"Sure I can dive. Next time you come to visit, I'll show you."

"Me, too," Allen said.

"You, too. But now I have to go see your Aunt Yelisa."

He carried Mary to Helen and stood her beside the chaise. He picked up his towel and Helen became very interested in Mary, patting her curls and hitching up her wet bathing suit.

"I've got to go now," Wesley told Helen. "The boys are still in the pool. Are you going to lifeguard or shall I get them out?"

"I've managed without your help for a good many years, Wesley," she said coldly. "I think you can leave my children's welfare to me."

Wesley spoke softly but with emphasis. "Well, be sure you watch Mary especially carefully; she's been jumping in."

"Thanks a lot for teaching her that."

As Wesley entered the offices of Mackenzie Mercury, Yelisa's secretary, Faye Morris, looked up and smiled at him. She came to the counter. "May I help you?"

"I have an appointment with Miss MacKenzie at eleven-thirty," he answered. "Wesley Callaghan."

"If you'll wait for just a moment, I'll tell her you're here." Faye went to her desk and picked up the phone. A moment later she put it down and said, "Go right in, Mr. Callaghan."

Wesley went behind the counter and through the door Faye indicated. Yelisa was already halfway across the room. She smiled happily and threw her arms around him. They kissed. And kissed again.

Yelisa leaned her head back to look into his eyes. "Hi, Wesley."

"Hi."

"It's a wonderful day." She took a pair of coveralls off the coat rack and held it out to him. Wesley looked at her quizzically. "Mercury's poisonous," she explained.

She pulled her own coveralls on and Wesley put his on. When they were completely enveloped in dark blue, with hard hats, Yelisa led the way to the headrig. The operator brought the elevator cage up for them and Yelisa took Wesley's hand as they went down into the depths of the mine. When the cage stopped, they were both perspiring freely. The foreman came to meet them and led the way to where the men were working, loading the ore cars. The foreman and Yelisa talked for a moment and the foreman went back to his work, supervising the drilling so explosives could be placed for detonation later in the afternoon.

Yelisa pointed out the various kinds of rock and minerals. "There's another vein that drifts off that direction. That's where we'll go when we get the ventilating shaft finished."

Wesley picked up a chunk of red ore. "It's hard to believe that this stuff yields liquid metal."

"Come on, we'll go up and see the plant."

Wesley tossed the ore into one of the cars as they went past and was delighted to get up on the surface again. Yelisa led the way into the plant and they were immediately deafened by the noise of the ore-crushing and other machinery. Yelisa didn't try to explain the operation, they just walked along, avoiding the working men, looking at everything. It was cooler than the mine but still plenty warm.

Once outside again, Yelisa said, "Wow, let's shed these duds."

They removed the protective clothing and Yelisa folded it so it wouldn't contaminate her tee-shirt and went back toward the office. As they passed the wash house, Yelisa went inside and put the soiled clothes in a big, covered bin. She washed her hands and Wesley followed her example.

"I don't see how the miners take that heat day after day," Wesley said.

"Some of them really love the work. I suppose most of them just tolerate it as way to make a living, though."

"Do you spend much time down there?"

"I'm in and out every two or three days. The superintendent and the engineer do most of the work concerning the actual production."

"You're the executive? From whom all orders flow?"

"Right. I am the boss lady."

They entered the office just as the noon whistle blew and everything shut down. Wesley stood aside so Faye could get past the counter and out the door, then followed Yelisa into her private office. He walked around the room, inspecting the wall charts, the views from the windows, the ore samples, and finally sat behind her desk. Yelisa stood and watched him.

"I just wondered how it all looked from your viewpoint," he told her.

"I know."

He stood up. 'What are your plans for lunch?"

"I'm not going home, if that's what you're thinking. Helen's leaving this afternoon, thank God, and I'm not going home until she's gone."

"Let's have lunch at the café, then."

"I know," Yelisa said with sudden excitement. "Let's go out to Richmond and have a picnic. We can get stuff for the lunch at Service Creek."

"Richmond?"

"It's a ghost town a few miles south of here. Come on!"

She linked her arm in his and propelled him out the door and to her car.

"Maybe we ought to take the pickup," Wesley suggested.

"Okay. Did you bring Jack?"

"Yeah, he's here somewhere." He opened the door and whistled. Jack came running up and jumped into the cab, wagging his tail happily.

They stopped at the little country store at Service Creek on the John Day River and bought their picnic. Yelisa pointed out the turn to Richmond and they stopped in a grove of skinny poplar trees. They sat on the tailgate with the picnic between them as they ate and drank beer, and watched Jack racing around pretending to chase jackrabbits.

The buildings were scattered except for a row of shops where they were parked. The church was still standing and the old schoolhouse. A little beyond the town site was a working ranch with its house and outbuildings.

"Isn't it lovely?" Yelisa asked.

"Why is it here? Surely there were never enough people in the county to justify two towns this close to each other."

"I don't really know. I've been visiting it all my life and I never thought about it. But I think about the people who lived here and I wonder about them."

"Mmm-hmm. It's rattlesnake country."

"Occasionally we get one right in town."

"This is where I show off."

He went to the cab and came back buckling on a heavy gunbelt with a Colt .45 in the holster. He wore it like an old-time gunfighter, low on his hip and tied down.

Yelisa laughed. "Oh, please, Mr. Earp, save me."

"Have no fear, ma'am," Wesley said, lowering his voice a couple of octaves. "I shall defend you. To the death, if need be."

"We shouldn't make fun of him. I know they say he took bribes from prostitutes, but he really was brave and he lived up to his own code."

"Even at the risk of his life. All right, we'll consider Wyatt a hero, with certain reservations."

"Doc Holliday was even less heroic than Wyatt but I like him better. He was so damn devil-may-care."

"He got off some pretty good quotes, too. 'If it had been me, it wouldn't have been an attempted stage robbery; I'd have robbed it.'"

Yelisa laughed. They wandered hand-in-hand to look at the old buildings. Jack returned to them now and then, only to race away again. The doors were locked but they peered in the windows and imagined the rooms populated with their long-ago inhabitants. Yelisa tried to imagine what it would be like to have to wear long skirts and petticoats in that dust and heat instead of jeans and a tee-shirt. They returned to the row of shops and, after checking for snakes, sat on the covered walk.

Yelisa pointed to the northeast. "About twelve miles over that way is where my great-grandfather first discovered the mercury. He and another cowboy were branding some stock and when they went to put the fire out, they noticed

110

the mercury in a little pool on one side. It was several years before they got around to finding out exactly what it was and started to develop the mine. The other cowboy drifted away just as things were starting to jell and he never turned up again. Great-grandpa didn't know if he had any family or where they would be. So the MacKenzies got it all. That was back in the eighteen-sixties when gold and silver were booming all over the west."

"Mercury is used in gold and silver mining?"

"Not in the mining, in the reduction. And not so much anymore. Mercury is too toxic and the long-term environmental damage is too great. People are finding other, better ways to process the ore."

"Are you a college graduate?"

"Colorado School of Mines."

They sat together silently for a moment or two.

"I thought you were going to show off for me," Yelisa said.

"How can I? The snakes didn't show."

"Set up some targets. Use the beer cans."

"Only if you'll throw them. I will not shoot innocent, sitting beer cans."

"All right."

She dug the cans out of the lunch sack and threw them as high as she could, one at a time. Wesley started with a fast-draw technique but switched to simple target shooting. When the cans were hopelessly riddled, Yelisa gathered them up and tossed them back in the lunch sack.

"Not bad," she said. "I'm impressed. Can you do it with mirrors?"

"Mirrors, okay. Video recordings, no. I do not lend myself to anything cheap or vulgar."

Yelisa laughed. "Idiot. You know I mean shooting."

"Oh, shooting. No, I don't have time to practice trick shooting. I can twirl it a little, though."

Wesley demonstrated some fancy spins and slipped the .45 accurately into the holster at the end of a series of twirls.

They drove back to the office bantering and joking. Wesley parked in front of the building and left the motor running as he stepped out and held the door for Yelisa, telling Jack to stay. Yelisa gave him a brief but meaningful kiss and strode into the office.

Chapter 9

Monte, Robbie Chatham and Evan Evans had lunch together at Dightman's and met the other members of the band at the rehearsal hall afterwards. Robbie was a middle-aged woman and looked rather weather beaten in a tan colored dress and low heeled pumps. Evan was the photographer. He was about twenty-five and he wore his hair long and wavy about his shoulders. He carried his camera as if it were an extension of his arm and used it often, snapping candid photos of the group. The three bandsmen were fiddling with their instruments and bantering back and forth among themselves. Robbie and Monte were sitting a little apart from the others.

"You think he really means it?" Robbie asked.

"He's serious all right. I've never seen him like this before and you know Wesley and I go back a long way.'

"Tell me about his bride."

Monte grinned. "She ought to make good copy. She runs MacKenzie Mercury – and it's an important outfit – all by herself. She's really something to see. And sing? That girl could top the charts any time she felt like it. But she prefers to run her company. And she's got little old Wesley following her around looking like a whipped pup."

"So he's fallen for someone at last. Probably the best thing that could happen to him. If she cares for him."

"Seemingly, she does. Looks at him like she was a boat and he was the ocean."

Robbie asked sharply, "A fan?"

"Doesn't look like it, not to me. She's not a clinger. It don't look to me like she's going to roll over a play dead for him."

"I can't wait to meet her."

Wesley came in and walked up behind Monte.

"Oh, she's something, all right," Monte said.

"Who's something?" Wesley wanted to know.

Robbie stood and they hugged one another.

"Good lord, Wesley," she exclaimed, "I always said you were the best looking man in show business and you're looking better than ever."

"Thanks, Robbie. You've been doing some good for a lot of people since we worked together in the old days."

"Aw, shucks, it's nothing."

They sat down and Robbie waved for Evan to join them.

"Monte was just telling me about your fiancée," Robbie said. "Can we get some pictures of you together? Maybe in her office or that big Victorian mansion Monte was telling me about."

"That will be for Yelisa to say."

Evan ambled up to shake hands with Wesley, who rose for the formality. Then the photographer sat with his arms across the back of the chair as Robbie made the introduction.

"Wesley, this is Evan Evans, positively the world's primo photographer."

"It's a pleasure, Wesley. I've always liked your music."

"Thanks. I wish I could say something nice about your work but I'm a little out of touch."

"When you see yourself as photographed by me, you'll find plenty of nice things to say."

"I'd like to shoot outside, if it's all right with you."

"Such as where, outside?"

Wesley turned to Monte. "Have you been out to Richmond?"

"Virginia?" Monte asked, surprised and puzzled.

"Some folks sure are ignorant. No, it's a ghost town a few miles south of here. I think it would make a hell of a backdrop for stills of the band."

Evan frowned. "Could be. Especially if you all look like cowboys. On the run. Real sinister, maybe. Let me think about it."

115

Robbie said, "I'll need an extensive interview. Your fans will want to know what you've been doing. And make it interesting, for heaven's sake."

"No problem. I think I've stored up enough color to get us started."

"I'll have to interview Miss MacKenzie and we'll need some shots of the two of you together."

"I'll talk it over with her. But it's strictly up to her, Robbie. If she wants to be splashed all over the fan mags, okay. If she says no, it's final."

"Well, a beautiful bride would be an asset, Wesley. But it was hard enough to get you to do things any way but yours in the old days – now I expect it's impossible."

Monte chimed in. "Pretty near."

Wesley agreed. "Yeah. Listen, why don't you and Evan sit in on this rehearsal? That'll give you a chance to see how we're working, and get acquainted with the new guys. Or do you already know them?"

"Jimmy I know slightly but I hadn't met Gary before today. Barney hasn't changed much. And Monte's just as raunchy as ever."

Wesley called the band to order and they all sat looking at him expectantly as he adjusted his guitar strap. They played for three hours, changing arrangements, suggesting new material and alterations to the old. Robbie was delighted to see how well they worked together and that the new material was entirely worthy of her best efforts in publicity.

While the rehearsal was under way, Yelisa was at Trudy's. Trudy had opened the trailer door sullenly. Yelisa explained who she was and Trudy invited her in, half reluctantly, half eagerly.

Yelisa was appalled by the trailer's condition. There were dirty dishes and clothes everywhere. It hadn't been swept or dusted in a long time and the windows were grimy. One was broken and had a piece of cardboard taped over the hole. Yelisa sat down on the only chair that didn't have clothes thrown in it. Trudy pushed a tangle of clothes and towels aside and sat on the couch.

"What exactly do you want, Miss MacKenzie?" she asked with a nasty little laugh.

"This is kind of difficult, Miss Allen."

"Mrs. Mrs. Allen."

'Mrs. Allen."

"You've never been married, have you, Miss MacKenzie?"

"No. No, I haven't." Yelisa couldn't help a soft, slight smile. "Not yet."

Trudy's voice sharpened. "What do you want?"

"Wesley says the baby you claim to be carrying isn't his and I came to ask you why you're staying here telling people it is."

Trudy blinked. Then she laughed. "Is poor old Wesley nervous?"

"No. We aren't nervous, Mrs. Allen. You aren't hurting either one of us. We'd just rather you went back to L.A. instead of spreading lies here."

"The baby is Wesley's," Trudy said venomously. "The baby is Wesley's and I'm going to make him take care of me and his baby. That's why I'm still in Fossil. And a better named town I never saw."

Yelisa smiled. "I didn't think you liked it much. If it's just money you're after, maybe we can work something out."

"No, it's not just money. Although it won't look very good for me to be on welfare while you and Wesley are living it up in your mansion. It might be embarrassing for you."

"Yes, it might. Look, why don't you be reasonable? You know that Wesley isn't the father of your child. Why not let us help you get back to L.A. where you'd much rather be anyway, and leave us alone?"

"Maybe you believe Wesley when he denies this baby, but it's his all right. He can't dump me and walk away scot free. And money isn't the only way to make him pay."

"I see. You're hoping to make it so hot for him here that he'll leave me and move on. I'm sorry for you, Mrs. Allen."

"Don't you dare pity me," Trudy said furiously.

"Nothing you can do will change things between Wesley and me. When is your baby due?"

"You'd like to know that, wouldn't you?"

"Oh, not the way you mean. No, if you're going to ignore facts and cause trouble by lies and innuendo, telling me the date won't help me. I just want to know how long we're apt to be saddled with you."

"I intend to make Wesley suffer the way he's made me suffer and he's got to provide for me and the baby."

Yelisa smiled. "Let's be honest, just between the two of us. You haven't suffered at all on Wesley's account except, possibly, from hurt pride. However, for the baby's sake and because it wouldn't look right to the people we have to live with, I'm prepared to pay your expenses – within reason – until the baby's born or until you leave Fossil. If you decide to leave, I'll give you a lump sum to see you through the next year. If you stay, I'll tolerate you just until the baby's born. If you try to stay after that, I'll find a way to get you out. And don't think I can't."

"Rich bitch. Just because you've got money, you think you can get away with murder. But Wesley will have to acknowledge this baby or the publicity will wreck his comeback."

"I don't think so. I think you'd better take my offer."

"I'm going to file a paternity suit against Wesley. I don't want charity, I want my rights."

"If you really think your chances of winning a court battle are good, go ahead. But don't count on it. A simple little blood test can probably clear Wesley without ever going to court."

"Get out! Get out and leave me alone!" Trudy jumped to her feet, caught up a china kitten from the coffee table and flung it against the wall. It shattered and she looked around for something else to throw.

Yelisa stood up and looked at the other woman for a moment. "You really are pathetic, you know."

As Yelisa went out the door, a china elephant crashed against the wall. In the car on the way home, she reflected on the scene with Trudy. She didn't think Trudy would file suit but she recognized that her spitefulness would probably keep her in Fossil unless they could think of a way to dislodge her.

When she got home, Wesley was in the upper sitting room, lying on the sofa, relaxed and listening to Mozart's "Clarinet Concerto in A Major." He looked up as she came into the room and sat up to make room for her beside him. Yelisa sat and swung her legs onto the sofa so she could turn and be cradled across his lap with her head on his chest. He brushed his lips across her forehead. The music ended but neither of them wanted to move or change it.

"I saw Trudy today," Yelisa said after a while.

"And?"

"She's lovely."

"Beauty is as beauty does."

"Yes. She cried and carried on and said all sorts of wild things. However, there seems to be no doubt that she's pregnant. It's beginning to show."

"What did you talk her into?"

"Nothing," Yelisa admitted ruefully. "She says she's going to slap a paternity suit on you. And that you won't dare fight it because the publicity would wreck your comeback."

"Everything's so damned upside-down, I'm not sure it wouldn't help."

"The worst case, as I see it, is this: if she wins a paternity suit, you'll have to fork over some cash, either a settlement or support payments. Since cash is not a problem, why don't we pay her now and skip the suit? She says she isn't after money, but she'd take it."

'It would be admitting her story is true. And it isn't."

"There is that, of course. We might make a settlement conditional to her leaving the state and not giving interviews."

"She'd leave, maybe, but I don't see her keeping her mouth shut."

"I don't either, really."

"Robbie's in town," Wesley remarked after a little pause.

"Robbie? Oh, the publicity wizard."

"They want some shots of you."

"What on earth for?"

"Don't you read the fan mags? Star weds beautiful young executive. With a picture of you in a white satin gown, standing beside the retorts. Are you kidding? You'd be on top in a week."

"But I'm already on top. MacKenzie Mercury is one of the most efficient operations of its kind in the entire United States. I have a plaque on my wall that says so. Presented by 'Mines and Mining Magazine' in the hope that I'd take out some really important ad space. My picture was on the cover, too."

"I'll bet they sold more magazines that month than ever before or since."

"Well, it's not exactly 'People Weekly,' you know. I'm afraid only people in the industry saw it. But it didn't hurt the business any. In fact, we got some new accounts. Mainly out of curiosity, I think."

"Are they still with you?"

"Sure. We really are efficient."

"We're going out to Richmond tomorrow to take some stills. What shall I tell Robbie about you? She wants to talk with you, too. Inside stuff."

"Why not? It might be fun. I'll have to work part of the day but it doesn't matter which part. We'll have everything arranged for the double shift to start Monday. You wouldn't believe what it takes just to hire one extra shift. And, of course, there's our wedding to plan. I'm not going to have time to buy a new dress. You don't mind, do you?"

"You look wonderful," he said, kissing her throat.

"Do you listen to classical music a lot?"

"Some. There are some composers I don't much care for. But some of the others are so good – the music makes me feel like church should but usually doesn't. To think of people being able to write and play music like that. It's almost holy." He stared into the distance with reverence in his face.

"You're a very complicated man, aren't you?"

"Isn't everybody complicated?"

"I don't think so." She slipped her hand inside his shirt. "Should I wear anything special for the photo session tomorrow?"

"Are you sure you want to do it? Because it can't be undone. Once Robbie's blitz hits the press, if people like us, your privacy is going to be practically nonexistent."

"In Wheeler County? No one would come here just to bug me. And the people already here already know all about me. All about us."

"I suppose," Wesley agreed doubtfully.

"Do you want me to do it?"

"Yeah. I want you to do it but I don't want the responsibility if it doesn't turn out right. I don't want to think that I talked you into it."

"All right, that's settled. What shall I wear?"

"You realize this might take most of the day and involve a dozen wardrobe changes."

"Not for me. Robbie can have her pictures if she takes them when she has the chance. Will the yellow silk shirt be okay? Or are you going for contrast and wearing evening clothes in the ruins? I have a terrific evening gown."

"It's an idea. We're thinking of a definite western theme for the show and the album so we'll just wear jeans and western shirts. The yellow silk will be perfect."

"Okay." Yelisa grinned rather guiltily. "Did you know there's a rodeo this weekend?"

"Sure. How could I miss it?"

"Wouldn't Robbie like some shots of you bronc riding?"

"On my wedding day? She'd sell her soul for them. Or my soul."

"I really think it's too good a chance to pass up."

"It's probably too late to sign up," Wesley said hopefully.

"Well, yes and no. It was for the parade. But I signed you up for saddle bronc and bull riding."

"I'll be killed," he exclaimed. "I'll be worse than killed, I'll be disemboweled."

"There, now, don't take on so. The rodeo committee can't afford really good stock. It'll be pretty tame."

"And where will you be while I'm getting my brains bashed in?"

"I'll be sitting on the fence, cheering for my man."

"That first night I saw you, I should have turned right around and walked away. Just walked away."

Yelisa kissed him sweetly. "You know you're glad you didn't."

Chapter 10

Yelisa woke early Sunday morning and lay for a while watching Wesley sleep. Finally her reluctance to disturb him was overcome by her wish to be fresh and sweet for him when he did wake. She slipped out of bed and went down the hall to one of the guest bathrooms so her shower wouldn't bother him. She went to her dressing table and applied a light coat of lipstick and eye shadow. When she turned toward the bed she was surprised to see Wesley propped on one elbow, watching her appreciatively. He'd evidently made his own ablutions for his hair was combed and he was freshly shaved.

"Good morning," she said. And then, to tease him, "You'd better get up quickly, we have a lot to do today."

Wesley pretended to have forgotten. "We have?"

"Today's the day you show me how to ride buckin' horses and bulls," she said with a big grin.

"Oh, hell!" he burst out. "I forgot to order flowers for the bride."

Yelisa laughed delightedly, threw the bedclothes back and stretched out at full length on his body. "Oh, Wesley, I'm so happy!"

Wesley was amazed at the mingled passion and tenderness that flooded his being. He hadn't known that he could feel like that. Wanting to drown in the curves and the soft, glossy waves of her hair and at the same time wanting to shield her from himself lest he grow too rough in his need of her.

"Yelisa. So you really are going to do it? You haven't taken the good advice you've been given to leave me while there's time?"

"You won't escape that way. We're supposed to be at Reverend Allison's study at one-thirty, and I intend to be there. You, of course, will suit yourself."

"Knowing that Agnes will be around with her twenty-gauge? I'll be there."

Yelisa sat up, astride his body. He reached up and gently touched her breasts. She smiled down at him and buried her face against his neck. Wesley's heart sang. Loving her gave him the greatest pleasure he'd ever experienced and knowing she was still capable of that sweet shyness heightened his desire.

Wesley took the Mercedes and drove into town to roust the florist out to put together a bouquet for Yelisa. While he was doing that, she prepared herself for her bridal day. It was a good thing Helen wasn't coming, she thought. Helen would have a lot to say about suitability if she could see Yelisa's substitution for a wedding gown. The pantsuit was light green, cut western style with deeply pointed yokes. The shirt was lighter green satin, striped with cream, with mother-of-pearl buttons. Her hat had a band of green feathers. She paused often to look at the emerald on her left ring finger and once or twice she was sentimental enough to kiss it.

She was out on the porch waiting for him when Wesley drove up. There was plenty of time before one-thirty so he joined her. He carried a big bundle done up in green florists' paper. She watched him critically as he mounted the steps and walked to where she sat in the swing, Jack at her feet. He undeniably moved well, she thought. And she liked his shirt. A little gaudy for a wedding perhaps, but there wouldn't be any chance to change before the rodeo and it was perfect for that. It was royal blue and made so that the front, instead of simply opening in a straight line, was cut in the shape of a large star and buttoned on the star points. Good theatre, she thought.

Wesley presented the flowers with a flourish and sat beside her as she tore the wrapping off. It was an enormous Victorian nosegay of pink and yellow roses with sprays of stephanotis.

"It's beautiful, Wesley," she said, holding it against her cheek.

"Yeah, the florist had to take it apart a couple of times before we were satisfied with it."

Yelisa laughed. "Before 'we' were satisfied with it?"

"Well, I reckon I was harder to please than she was. I'm glad you like it."

Yelisa took the two gold rings from her pocket and handed him the smaller one. "You'd better take this one. It would look pretty silly if I had to dig it out in the middle of the ceremony."

Wesley held the ring in the palm of his hand and looked at it a long time. "We should have had something engraved in them. Eternal love or something like that."

"I don't know. I kind of like the idea of a plain gold band with no elaborate promises. This way we're free to love one another without feeling we've mortgaged the future, or have anything to live up to."

"I don't think I quite understand," Wesley said.

"Maybe I don't either, quite. But, okay, it's like this. If we make a lot of extravagant promises about eternal love or always sharing everything, we've already set up barriers between us. I hope our love is eternal but I don't want that phrase looming ahead of me like a rock on a foggy coast. If we find we can't share everything, and I'm sure we can't, I don't want either of us to feel guilty or resentful because a promise has been broken. Let's take life as it comes, free and unfettered."

"I think you are the only person I've ever known who regards marriage as freedom. Are we really not going to allow it to constrict us? Is it possible without growing apart and losing touch with each other?"

"I think so," Yelisa said softly, smiling at him. "Or else we wouldn't be making the experiment. Oh, yes, Wesley, our marriage is going to be different from any you've ever seen before."

"Thank God."

'Do you mean that you thought it would mean less freedom, a decreasing horizon, but you were going to do it anyway? Why?

"I need you," he answered simply, looking into her eyes intently.

"Yes, I see you do," she said slowly. "But, please, Wesley, please don't let your need lead you into making sacrifices. Because every sacrifice eventually means resentment, usually on both sides. Don't let us ever make victims of one another."

"Victims," he repeated. He looked out across the hills. "We'll be two whole, healthy people, Yelisa. Between the two of us, we can keep on an even keel."

"I feel like someone ought to say, 'You may kiss the bride.'"

"Yeah. I think we just said all the important things."

"I know." Yelisa smiled deprecatingly at him. "But something in me wants the traditional ceremony. You don't really mind, do you?"

"I don't. And it's time to go. You have my ring and I have yours. You have your posies. Is Aggie coming with us?"

"No, she went with her friends a couple of hours ago. She had some preserves and flowers and a cake at the fair she wanted to see if she'd won anything on. She'll meet us at the manse."

They stood and Wesley took her in his arms. "I love you," he said.

Yelisa answered softly. "I love you."

The Reverend Allison was a quick-moving, quick-talking man. He bustled them into his study where Mrs. Allison and Agnes were waiting. Mrs. Allison was a placid lady, tall and blond, who welcomed them with a sweet smile. She and the minister had known Yelisa since they'd come to Fossil fourteen years earlier and they'd grown fond of her. They were inclined to look askance at Wesley in spite of Aggie's earlier assurances that he was good for Yelisa. Mrs. Allison kissed Yelisa's cheek and shook hands with Wesley. The Reverend shook hands with them both. Agnes stood near the desk and beamed at everyone.

The ceremony took only a few minutes, Reverend Allison read the vows so quickly that Yelisa almost lost the sense of them once or twice and Wesley was glad of the training he'd had in learning new lyrics because it helped him grasp the parts he was to repeat. After Wesley kissed the bride, there was another round of hugging and kissing and hand-shaking.

"Where are you going for your honeymoon, dear?" Mrs. Allison asked Yelisa.

Yelisa grinned. "We don't have time for one. Wesley has to leave with the band next weekend and I have to stay here and get the kinks ironed out of the second shift we're starting tomorrow."

The Reverend was astonished. "But my dear young people, the honeymoon is very important. You need the time alone to get adjusted to your new life together."

Wesley was delighted to see Yelisa blush. Agnes tightened her lips and resolved to drop a hint to Mrs. Allison regarding the Reverend's tactlessness.

"It won't be all that different, sir," Wesley said.

Mrs. Allison caught her husband's eyes and shook her head at him ever so slightly. He remembered then that he'd heard some talk that Wesley and Yelisa hadn't waited for the formality of marriage to begin their life together. His wife relieved his confusion by bringing in a white-frosted cake with a little plastic bride and groom on it.

"I knew you hadn't planned a reception, Yelisa, and I hope you don't mind, but I felt I just had to see you cut the cake."

"Oh, Mrs. Allison, how lovely of you." Yelisa's eyes were suddenly moist. How nice people were. She thought of the reception her mother would have given her and the pride her father would have had in her on this day. It never occurred to her that her parents would find Wesley anything but the perfect husband for her.

Wesley was pleased for Yelisa's sake. He could see that she was very moved and his heart warmed to these rather doddery, elderly people. Agnes wiped a tear away and went into the kitchen to help Mrs. Allison bring in the plates and coffee. When everything was assembled, Yelisa and Wesley cut the cake and exchanged the traditional bites. They drank the coffee they didn't want and ate the cake that was too sweet and carried the little plastic bride and groom away with them. Agnes refused a lift to the fairgrounds, saying she was meeting friends at a house on the next street.

Wesley and Yelisa drove down a side street and parked in the shade of a big old poplar tree. They kissed a good deal and exulted in their marital bliss. At length they returned more or less to sanity, although the kissing went on at intervals.

"It's time we got to the rodeo," Yelisa said reluctantly.

Wesley started the car. "You're mighty anxious to see me get broke in half, ma'am."

Yelisa laughed. "I was right, Wesley. We've been married less than an hour and I'm already having the most fun of my life. Being married to you is entertaining."

The Wheeler County Fairgrounds were small, as befitted such a small (in population) county, but they were crowded with enthusiastic rodeo fans. A small carnival was set up and a couple of food booths stood behind the grandstand. The announcer's booth was a rickety-looking little box suspended from the ceiling of the grandstand and the P.A. system left a lot to be desired.

Monte and the rest of the band were mingling with the crowd, Monte and Jimmy with the girls they'd taken up with in the last weeks. Trudy was there with Tom Plank. Robbie and Evan were standing near Yelisa who was perched on the fence watching exuberantly. Wesley was back of the chutes, waiting his turn to ride in the saddle bronc contest and watching the competition, all of whom were at least six or eight years younger than he.

Wade Filson completed his ride, the buzzer sounded and one of the pickup men swung him behind his cantle. Another rider caught the bronc and led him out of the arena.

Johnny Gardis had been the announcer for that rodeo for nearly thirty years. It was his one claim to distinction so he didn't mind that the P.A. system turned his voice tinny.

"A good ride, Wade," he said. "We'll have the results in just a few minutes. Our next cowboy is not only a champion bronc rider, he's a nationally famous singer. This is Wesley's wedding day, folks. He and Miss Yelisa MacKenzie were married this afternoon. Say hi to the folks, Mrs. Callaghan."

Yelisa waved her nosegay, smiling broadly. The applause was tremendous.

Wesley took his place in the chute, standing on the boards, straddling the bronc but above the saddle. The bronc was standing quietly and Wesley slipped into the saddle, took a firm grip on the rein,, held the other hand up high and nodded. The gate tender swung the gate wide and Wesley came out with his spurs well over the bronc's shoulders. After the first jump, the bronc wasn't particularly ferocious but Wesley spurred a fair ride out of him and stayed the full ten seconds.

Evan was taking pictures from every angle he could manage and got so excited that he ran out into the ring. The buzzer sounded but Evan was in the way of the pick-up men and Wesley was dumped. He rolled out of the way of the horse's hooves, picked up his hat, dusted it against his chaps and limped over to the gate, out of the arena. Yelisa swung around and jumped off the fence to join him.

"We've got an upset, folks," Johnny said. "Wade Filson's been disqualified. The judges say his off-side spur wasn't over the shoulder on that first jump. Tough luck, Wade."

The crowd made noises of sympathy and disappointment. Wade was a popular hometown cowboy.

"All right," Johnny continued, as a runner handed him a paper, "here it is: third place is Jim Sutton, second is Wesley Callaghan, and our first place winner is Greg Mattson. Congratulations, boys."

The crowd applauded heartily.

"Come on out," Johnny ordered. "The crowd wants another look at you bronc riders."

Wesley grabbed Yelisa by the arm and pulled her out with him. Jim and Greg and three or four others were lined up and a pretty teenage rodeo queen presented a silver buckle to Greg and kissed him. The photographer from the Condon paper was taking pictures and Evan was, too. The queen and the other cowboys left the arena and Wesley turned Yelisa in a deep back-bend and kissed her thoroughly. The crowd yelled its approval.

Wesley shouted, "I just wanted to be sure something still works."

Johnny laughed. "All right. In case you didn't hear that, folks, Wesley says he just wanted be sure something still works. That hurricane deck's no place for a man on his wedding day, huh, Wesley?"

Wesley and Yelisa had turned and were leaving the arena arm-in-arm but at Johnny's words, she turned back to grin and wave her bouquet at Johnny.

"When's the bull riding?" Wesley asked as he closed the gate behind them.

"Right after bareback."

"I hope there aren't many bareback riders,' he said fervently. "The quicker I get on that bull the better."

"What's the matter, starting to stiffen up?"

"In another hour, I won't be able to move."

Evan and Robbie intercepted them and a moment later a couple dozen people, mostly teens, came to ask for Wesley's autograph. He signed good-naturedly but Yelisa noticed he didn't ask what they wanted him to write.

"That was wonderful, Wes,' Robbie burbled. "Evan got some terrific shots. This is the kind of colorful stuff that ought to knock 'em dead. Better even than an affair with a lovely young starlet. Although that would be good, too."

Yelisa spoke a little dryly. "Everyone has his own point of view, I guess."

"I hope you're not going to expect this in every town we play," Wesley said.

Robbie grinned. "That would be splendid. I don't suppose most of them even have rodeos, though."

"Doesn't it mean anything to you people that I'm in intense pain and my insides are probably all busted up and I'm almost certainly not going to live to make a tour anyway?"

Even had been fiddling with his equipment instead of following the conversation. "Could you ride that horse again later, Wesley? I couldn't get all the angles I wanted. When the horse rears with his forefeet pawing the air, that would make a wonderful low-angle shot with you waving your arm like that."

"Look," Wesley said patiently, "if that horse kills me, it won't matter how great your low-angle shots are. I am through bronc riding."

Yelisa led the way to a covered pavilion where beer was sold. She bought four big plastic cups full and handed them around. Even took a couple of pictures.

Wesley said to Yelisa, "You get the idea? Once you become public property, you can't count on making a move without a photographer at your elbow. Not that I'm complaining, Evan. You're doing a fine job. I just want the girl to know what she's getting into."

Robbie signaled to Evan. "I think it's time for us to be tactful, and go and take pictures of the rest of the band."

Evan picked up his beer and followed her as she left the pavilion.

Wesley drank deeply and winced as he turned to face Yelisa. She grinned at him and promised to kiss the hurt place and make it well.

From Evan and Robbie's point of view, the bull riding was even better than the bronc riding. The Brahma bull was a lot more active than the horse had been. The buzzer finally sounded the eight-second mark and Wesley came off. The clown came toward the bull to give Wesley a chance to leave the arena but something went wrong with the clown's timing and he slipped under the bull's hooves. Wesley and the pick-up men ran toward the bull and Wesley distracted the animal while the others jumped off their horses and carried the clown out. Wesley leaped over the fence one jump ahead of the bull, who then trotted around, snorting fiercely. The crowd went wild cheering and Yelisa came running up to him.

"That was a close one," she said as she threw her arms around him.

"Middling," he answered, putting one arm around her shoulders. "Where's the clown?"

Evan ran up, still photographing. "My God, this is beautiful stuff."

Yelisa said to Wesley, "They took him to the E.M.T.'s truck."

Wesley limped his way to the emergency medical technician's truck, holding tightly to Yelisa's hand. He felt he could not bear it if the clown were badly injured just because of a publicity stunt. They found the clown was stretched out inside the truck, which was fitted out like an ambulance. The E.M.T., John Courtland, was palpating his abdomen. Wesley signed autographs and Evan took a couple of pictures while John immobilized the clown's arm with an air splint. Finally he stepped out of the truck.

"How is he?" Wesley asked.

"His right arm's broken, just a simple fracture, I think, and he's got some minor abrasions and contusions. I'll take him to the clinic for observation and to get that arm set, but he's okay."

The clown called, "Hey, is that Wesley Callaghan out there?"

Wesley stepped to the open door of the truck. "Yeah."

"Come in here a minute."

Wesley mounted the step and groaned as he heaved his body into the vehicle. "Sorry about all this."

The clown was indignant. "Sorry! You're sorry! I don't believe it. I screw up my job so I have to be rescued by the man that I'm supposed to rescue and he's sorry."

"Well," Wesley said reasonably, "if I hadn't been out there, you wouldn't have been, either."

"Ah, you're hopeless. I just wanted to thank you for saving my ass."

"You're welcome. I'd better get out of here so they can get you to the clinic."

The E.M.T. spoke as Wesley descended from the truck. "I think I'll wait until the bull riding's over before I transport him. I may be needed again."

Yelisa touched his arm. "Wesley, listen. They're calling your name. Come on."

They crossed back to the arena where all the bull riders were lined up waiting to hear who won. The crowd and the cowboys applauded as Wesley entered the arena. Yelisa went up to the announcer's booth.

Johnny asked over the P.A., "How's he doing, Wesley?"

Wesley shouted the answer. "Okay, just a broken arm."

"All right, folks," Johnny said. "Ormand's got a broken arm, that's all. Let's hear a nice round of applause for Wesley Callaghan for preventing a bad stomping for Ormand."

Wesley waved his hat and pointed to the two pick-up men who were leaning against the stall fronts, holding their horses' reins, and watching Wesley cynically. Johnny picked up on Wesley's meaning.

"And another round of applause for Bud Jackson and Phil Marston. These boys are just as important to the success of the rodeo as the riders and clowns. And they've done an outstanding job here today."

Bud and Phil were surprised but they grinned and tipped their hats politely to the audience who obliged with renewed applause for them.

"Okay," Johnny said when he could be heard again, "we have the results of the bull riding event. Third place is Wade Filson; second place, Greg Mattson; and our first place winner is Wesley Callaghan."

The crowd approved noisily and the rodeo queen brought the silver buckle out, presented it to Wesley and kissed him very prettily.

Johnny could be heard over the P.A. before he was ready to announce anything. "What? Oh." Then he used his announcer's voice, "Folks, we've got a guest here in the announcer's booth. Mrs. Wesley Callaghan wants to say a word."

Evan, who had been photographing the trophy presentation, turned to focus on Yelisa.

"I'd like to toss my bouquet. Here, boys, the one who catches it will be the next one married."

She threw the nosegay down to the cowboys in the arena and they grabbed at it eagerly. Wade Filson made a high jump for it and brandished it over his head. He looked for his girl in the stands and beckoned madly. The crowd laughed delightedly.

Yelisa drove home to find Jack waiting plaintively on the front porch. He wagged his tail and followed them anxiously as Wesley hobbled out of the Mercedes and Yelisa hurried around to help him up the steps. He groaned as he straightened up and Jack whined and came to look up at him worriedly. Wesley stroked his head and reassured him. Yelisa put her arm around Wesley's waist and he put his arm lightly across her shoulders. They went slowly up the steps and into the house.

"I always heard that men were babies when they were hurt or sick," Yelisa said as they went up the stairs.

"Women always say that when they're feeling particularly effervescent in the presence of pain and agony."

"Probably," Yelisa laughed. "A hot bath and massage ought to help."

"Yes, ma'am, I'd be mighty grateful if you'd tend my wounds and nurse me back to health."

While Wesley soaked in the hot bath, Yelisa showered in one of the guest bathrooms and put on a jersey hostess gown that was cut to a deep V and buttoned down the front. She lightly touched her lips and eyes with makeup, folded the bedclothes completely off the bed and sat in the chaise to wait for Wesley. She thought back over her wedding day and smiled to herself. How scandalized Helen would be. How absolutely fitting and appropriate to the two of them the day had actually been. She knew she would always look back on this day with love and laughter. What fun it would be to tell their children and grandchildren about the rodeo their dad and grandpa had ridden in on his wedding day. And how their mom and grandma had thrown her bridal bouquet to the cowboys instead of to a gaggle of bridesmaids. The Allisons were dear people. It had been lovely of them not to lecture or be shocked that she and Wesley had cohabited before the wedding. And the cake. She'd left the little bride and bridegroom in the car. Well, it would be all right there until later.

Wesley emerged from the tub relaxed and nearly boneless. Yelisa steered him to the bed and, by judicious nudges and tugs, arranged him on his stomach. She fetched a jar of crème from her dressing table and smoothed great dollops on his back. She massaged smoothly and rhythmically, beginning with his neck and finishing with his toes.

Wesley had never been so completely at ease and happy. There was nothing in Yelisa that he had to protect himself against; nothing in himself to guard against revealing. Well, there was a lot in his past that he didn't intend to tell her about, but there was nothing that he would be shattered by if she did find out. He was astonished at the depth of intimacy that was possible between them. Total acceptance.

"This is almost worth getting the hell pounded out of me," he said.

"'All Shook Up' Takes on a whole new meaning, huh?"

"Also, "A Whole Lot of Shakin' Goin' On.'"

"Turn over so I can do your front."

"That sounds promising," he said huskily.

Wesley rolled onto his side and contemplated her. Her hair was loose and fell in waves, framing her face, which was soft and serene in the long shadows of evening. He unfastened the buttons of her gown and she slipped it off her shoulders.

"Come here, Mrs. Callaghan," he whispered.

Chapter 11

As Wesley entered the rehearsal hall, which was actually the Home Ec Building of the fairgrounds, Monte and the others were messing around with an old rock and roll tune. It reminded Wesley of a rockabilly song he'd always liked and he asked for it. They played it while Wesley sang and it came across fine, with only a little adjusting to do.

The drummer, Barney, laid his sticks down and pulled a folding chair around to complete the circle. "It's great to have you back, Wes."

Gary, who played various guitars, agreed. "Yeah. Now watch us hit those charts."

Jimmy pushed his chair back from his keyboard and asked, "What with?"

"Our music," Gary answered blankly.

Barney got Jimmy's point. "Jimmy's right. Our music is all the old stuff. We'll need some new material. Wesley's or someone's."

Monte spoke. "How about it, Wes? You got any new material for us?"

Wesley looked around the circle. "Yeah, I've got some stuff I've never published."

"We've got some material we haven't used, too," Barney said. "Never seemed to get just the right arrangements."

"We'll work on 'em," Wesley said. "Now, we've got to be ready for Klamath County in about a week. We can't work out a whole new program but we can do a little changing around. Since Monte's willing for me to take over as lead vocalist, I guess it's okay with all of you?"

They all made various gestures and noises indicating that they agreed.

Monte went further. "Take your old job back. Lead the singing and the band."

The others nodded and Wesley weakened. It was what he wanted. Wanted real bad, too. "All right," he said. "I will."

He named a song and they all took their places to work out the arrangement.

Wesley was sitting on the wide front steps, strumming a guitar as he waited for Yelisa to come home. Jack was lying beside him. Wesley was playing a beautiful melody, stopping to re-work a phrase now and then, but playing with increasing confidence. Yelisa drove in and stepped out of the Mercedes. Jack nearly turned himself inside out in his joy at seeing her. She stopped to pat the dog. Wesley looked up at her and she sat down beside him. He set the guitar aside and took her hand in his. She smiled at him.

"It's all set," he told her. "I'm going to Klamath County with the boys and on through the rest of the gigs they've got set up this year. As the – now get this – as the leader. Are you impressed?"

"Very much so. Do you have to bale hay in the morning?"

Wesley nodded. "My last day. I'm kind of sorry. I have one day of freedom left."

"Freedom? What do you mean?"

"After tomorrow I'll be the leader of the band. If we're successful, I'll be a star again. It's much easier and simpler to be a ranch hand."

"You aren't doing it for me?" Yelisa asked anxiously.

"No. My reasons are entirely selfish. And I'll do it my way or not at all. But I've got to give it one more shot. My best shot."

"I know. That's what I feel, too. Putting on a double shift at the mine and the plant is a lot of work and Tom thinks it's the wrong approach."

"But it's your decision and your job and you love it."

'I love you for knowing that." She paused and added, "I have to work after dinner."

"Okay." He hesitated and said, "I told Monte he could announce our marriage tonight."

"After the rodeo, I'd think everyone already knows."

"I expect so. But he wants to and there's no harm in it. Unless you object?"

"No, of course not. Do you want me there?"

"I want you right by my side. If you finish your work reasonably early and you'd like to drop in, Monte wants us to do a cheek-to-cheek spotlight. And I'd like you to sing our special song with me."

"All right. Do I have to wear a dress?"

"Now, you know you're going to wear what you damn well please, why ask me?"

Yelisa laughed. "Come out to the barn with me."

Wesley put the guitar back in its case and they wandered off, hand-in-hand, Jack tagging along. A three-car garage stood behind a screen of shrubbery and the barn was beyond the garage, down a grassy path. There were two horses in the barn, Yelisa's palomino and a chestnut mare. Yelisa took the lead shank and halter and went into the chestnut's stall. She buckled on the halter and led the horse out to Wesley. Wesley ran his hands down the horse's flanks and legs.

"She's a beautiful animal," he said.

"I thought you'd like her. Her name's Frostbit on account of the white on the tips of her ears. She's my wedding present to you."

Wesley glanced at his watch. "We've got forty-five minutes till I'll have to get suited up. Let's go for a ride."

"The tack room's behind you."

Wesley tacked up with the heavy western equipment while Yelisa fetched her horse. He led

149

the mare out into the yard and mounted up. Yelisa followed and mounted her mare, then led the way up a trail into the forest. The trees opened out into a meadow which she used for a riding arena. There were a couple of jumps set up on one side and a circle worn in the grass near the center. The horses were a little skittish from being cooped up in their stalls and Jack was having a wonderful time trotting along, making friends with them.

Wesley tried out Frostbit's paces, side-stepping, backing, haunch-turning, and so forth. The mare was willing and Wesley was patient. Yelisa trotted her mare around the track a couple of times and loped toward the jumps. The mare took them easily and Yelisa went around again at a canter. Wesley warmed Frostbit up and took her over the jumps. Much to his satisfaction, she jumped eagerly and well. It was going to be fun to ride again.

Wesley sang lead on nearly every number that evening and the crowd loved him. He sang mostly their old country rock numbers mixed with country standards. Wesley had told the waitress not to reserve Yelisa's table because she would probably be late. It wasn't until the second set that she came in. She was wearing high heels and a halter-top dress with her hair piled up in loose waves. She looked ravishing.

A cowboy was sitting on the stool at the end of the bar but he slid off and with a friendly grin, motioned for her to sit there. She smiled her thanks and sat. Wesley had been watching her since she entered the room and, as the song ended, he handed his guitar to Monte and walked to the edge of the platform, holding out his hand for her to join him. She went up the steps and stood arm-in-arm with him in front of the microphone. The applause renewed as she waved at the crowd and Wesley waited for it to die down so he could be heard.

"Thank you," he said. "Thank you." He had to wait a little longer. "Thank you, we appreciate it." The applause finally stopped as the folks realized that he had something to say. "Monte told you about Miss MacKenzie's marriage to me."

The applause started up again, accompanied by calls of congratulations and a couple of ribald whistles.

"Yeah," Wesley agreed. "Thank you. We're pretty happy about it, too."

He signaled the band and they struck up the special song that was Wesley and Yelisa's. They sang it to each other and while the crowd was applauding, they went down to the dance floor and the band played a love song while they danced. They motioned for others to join them and few couples took the floor with them. After Wesley returned to the band platform, Yelisa danced every dance. Old friends congratulated her and an old boyfriend gazed soulfully into her eyes until she reminded him that he had a wife and four children at home. All in all, she enjoyed the evening very much, but she wasn't sorry when it ended and she and Wesley drove home and went up the steps in the starlight.

The last night of Robbie's stay in Fossil, Yelisa gave a party for her and the band. Evan had other commitments and had returned to L.A. a couple of days after the rodeo but he'd left dozens upon dozens of photos.

Agnes had cooked mountains of food and been prevailed upon to join the fun. The boys had elected not to bring dates; it would be a family affair with no fans and no outsiders. Yelisa and Wesley had collaborated on the drinks and outfitted a table with bottles and glasses and an ice bucket.

The party didn't get started until after the show at the Pastime so it was very late when Yelisa and Wesley stood at the piano with Robbie and Jimmy and looked at Evan's pictures. Yelisa studied one of the band in front of the row of shops in Richmond. Jack was in the picture, too, lying at Wesley's feet. There was a lot of laughter and everyone chattered convivially.

"Well, you don't look sinister, Wesley," Robbie said, looking from the pictures to the man. "I expect it's best to go with these. If we tried to get the effect, it'd go wrong. The public would sense its falseness. They so often do."

Jimmy held out a picture of Wesley being unloaded by the bull. "Here's one I like. I've always liked heroics mixed with farce."

Robbie snatched the photo. "Farce? The story of Wesley and the clown's rescue will create tremendous interest. People love to read about people who do things. This campaign is just full of the things people love: brides, clowns, courageous rescues, wealth, beautiful people. If I can't get this story splashed all over the press, I'll go to choppin' cotton for a living."

Yelisa laughed. "Do you know how to chop cotton?"

Wesley shook his head. "She doesn't even know what choppin' cotton is."

"All right, all right," Robbie protested. "But, look." She held up a photo of Wesley and Yelisa in the arena. "This one picture makes me want to find out about these people. And it'll strike the public the same way. They'll admire your looks and the way your jeans fit and then wonder why one of you's wearing dusty chaps and the other one's carrying a Victorian nosegay."

Wesley looked at her solemnly. "The boys and I'd better get enough material for a second album together, then."

"Are you kidding?" Robbie demanded excitedly. "Once this campaign gets rolling, when the first release hits about mid-chart, you'd better have the second album ready so we can release it as soon as the first one tops out. You'll have a

153

sell-out tour and we'll get another planned for next summer, at the stadiums. It'll probably have to be international."

Yelisa laughed. "You leave me breathless, Robbie, you go so fast."

"It sounds good," Wesley said, "and we'll go ahead with it, but don't expect a sold-out crowd every night. And don't build that clown thing up to be more than what actually happened."

Monte came over and sat at the piano. Yelisa sat on the bench beside him. He played a few bars of a sad, sweet melody.

"Well, Yelisa," he asked, "what do you think of it all?"

"It's exciting. It's going to be great fun."

"You know Robbie's going to play up the fact that you signed Wesley up to ride."

"Sure. Why not?"

"They'll twist it. Make you sound like an air-headed bitch with no soul."

"I suppose it could look like that," Yelisa said thoughtfully. "Wesley didn't mind."

"Hell, no. Wesley thinks it was a fine thing. He was delighted that you thought of it."

Yelisa yawned and covered it with her hand. "Excuse me." Then she laughed. "Did you see his face when that bronc come high rolling out of the chute?"

Monte grinned. "He looked like he was wishin' he'd practiced more and better, all right."

"I was almost sorry about signing him up to ride the bull, though." She yawned again. "I'm sorry I keep yawning."

"I don't suppose you stay up till three every night of the week."

"No, not usually. But this was our only chance to get together with Robbie and the whole band before she goes back tomorrow. And I wanted to get better acquainted with everyone."

"Well, you made a hit. It's lucky that Robbie likes you. You'll get a lot better press than if she didn't."

Yelisa laughed again. "Then I'm glad, too." She looked up at Wesley and said, "Play something soft and dreamy, would you. Monte? I want to go hold hands with Wesley."

Monte began to play as requested and Yelisa detached Wesley from Robbie, who went to the bar to freshen her drink. Wesley stood with his arm around Yelisa and sang to Monte's accompaniment. When the song was over, Monte stood up and people began to say their goodbyes.

Yelisa sat at her dressing table, brushing her hair. She was wearing a filmy black peignoir but hadn't bothered with the nightgown. Wesley was sitting in bed watching her.

"How's the second shift working out?" he asked.

Yelisa smiled at his reflection in the mirror. "It's meshing very nicely. Tom's being a little obstructive about the ventilating shaft but otherwise it's smooth."

"Good."

Yelisa put the brush down and wandered over to look out the window. The moon was waning and it was dark outside.

"Your wedding present is in my pants pocked," Wesley said.

Yelisa laughed. "I've never got over feeling like a little girl at the mere mention of presents. Where are they?"

She crossed the room to a chair where Wesley had tossed his clothes and picked up the pants. "I've always wanted to rifle a man's pants."

"It would be more fun with the man inside them," Wesley remarked.

"Not now, Wesley. You don't carry much, do you? I thought men were supposed to stuff their pockets full of all sorts of trash."

"That's it," Wesley said. "The envelope."

Yelisa tore it open. "What is it? It looks like a car title." She brought it over to the light and sat down beside Wesley to read it. "It's a plane! A Cessna Skyhawk SP."

"It's just a little four-seater. It'll do to see if you like flying or not. I had to order it but they promised it'd be here by Saturday."

"Saturday!" Yelisa exclaimed excitedly. "But where will we put it, Wesley? We don't have a hangar or landing strip or anything."

"Tomorrow you give Mr. Radzinski a call and tell him where you want the runway. He's all lined out to build it for you. It only needs to be a dirt strip."

"I wonder if that flat just below the mine would work?"

"I'd suggest you ask Vern Worsham to go out with you and look. I did a little checking and he's the best instructor in the area. You know him, don't you?"

"Vern? Sure. He took me to the prom one year."

"Maybe I'd better do some more checking."

Yelisa bent down to kiss him and then twirled across the room.

"I'm so excited. Isn't it funny how you can have wishes you don't even know about? I never thought about learning to fly but I believe I've always wanted to. Oh, Wesley, this is going to be great. When you're on tour or in L.A., I can fly to Portland and be with you in a matter of hours."

"Yeah, I know."

Yelisa sat beside him. "Wesley! You didn't buy this plane for me, you bought it for yourself."

He pulled her into his arms. "I told you I was selfish."

Chapter 12

There was a big sign painted on each side of the band's big black van that read, "Wesley Callaghan and Prowess." The van was standing in the driveway while Wesley, Monte, and Jimmy loaded Wesley's gear.

"Where's Yelisa?" Jimmy asked.

"At the mine," Wesley answered.

Jimmy stared. "You mean she isn't going to see you off?"

"She's coming down tonight," Wesley said, putting a suitcase in the roof rack.

"She flying?" Monte asked.

"Not by herself," Wesley said. "She's a quick study, but not that quick. An old friend is doing the piloting."

Jimmy shook his head. "You want to watch out for those old friends."

Monte looked at his watch. "Gary and Barney took off in the truck a couple of hours ago. We'd better get going so we'll be there in plenty of time to get the stage rigged."

As they were climbing into the van, Agnes came out on the porch carrying a fair-sized cardboard carton. "Wait a minute. Here."

Jimmy turned and went up a couple of steps. "What's this, Aggie?"

"Your lunch. There's milk in the thermos, fried chicken and green salad," she said, looking at Wesley. "I want to be sure you eat right, at least your first meal out."

Jimmy took the carton and looked inside. "Wow, Aggie, a veritable feast. Thanks. You take care of yourself, now."

Wesley ran up the steps and kissed her cheek. "Yeah. And take care of Yelisa, too."

They drove away then, leaving Agnes in the driveway, waving after them. Wesley, Monte, and Jimmy took turns driving to Klamath Falls. They stopped for lunch at the park in Bend. It was a pretty park with the Deschutes River running through it. Wesley had got used to home cooking and thought ruefully that he'd be getting un-used to it again right quick. Jimmy and Monte thoroughly enjoyed everything but Wesley fed his share of the salad to the ducks. He liked most other vegetables okay, but he'd never learned to like lettuce.

It wasn't a very interesting drive after Bend, just a hundred and fifty miles of jack pine. Some snow-covered peaks in the middle distance. And Klamath Lake was certainly big enough, if it wasn't particularly scenic. Wesley had driven his stint to Bend so he lay down on the bench seat in back and slept most of the way. He'd never found a good way to fold his long legs, though, so he didn't sleep in any great comfort.

They met Gary and Barney at the chain motel in downtown Klamath Falls where they had reservations. Wesley and Monte shared a room and next door Jimmy, Barney, and Gary shared another. Wesley and Yelisa would have a little time together before he and the boys needed to leave. Monte had said rather diffidently that Wesley might as well spend the time with Yelisa, he and the boys were used to rigging and packing without him. They had about four hours before they needed to get out to the fairgrounds so they all sacked out and Monte was soon fast asleep.

Wesley sat on one of the chairs by the window and missed Yelisa. He wondered how she felt alone in their room for the first time since…well, since the first time. She'd be at work, talking to Tom, maybe dictating letters, no, it was Saturday, Faye wouldn't be there. Maybe she'd asked the engineers to come in and discuss the mine. Or maybe there were problems in the plant and she had the foreman in. Probably she was just reading reports or signing letters or some other totally routine business.

Maybe she'd been able to get away early. Maybe she was home by now, changing for her trip. She often put some music on while she changed, she might be listening to him right now. Against all the copyright laws, she had recorded Agnes' copy of his one album. He'd been amazed when Monte told him it was still in print as a CD and had sent for one for her.

He thought about that amazement of his. Not very flattering to Monte and the boys. Monte and Barney had recorded many times – with Jimmy and Gary and with others. They hadn't had a number one hit but they'd made some good showings on the charts a time or two. He hoped they could all make the comeback. He felt good about it, confident, ready. But you never could tell about the music-buying public. Maybe they wouldn't like the mature Wesley; maybe the kid was the only Wesley they cared about. Well, it wouldn't be too long before he found out.

Yelisa had quite a collection of music. CDs, tapes, videos, even vinyl. Some of her favorites dated from way before her time. Crosby, for instance. That was probably her mother's influence. Gene Autry, too. He grinned to himself as he considered himself and the boys recording "Deep Purple" or "Sioux City Sue." Wonderful music but for another time, other musicians.

Wesley thought about putting a tennis court in behind the swimming pool. Funny, he didn't even know if Yelisa played tennis. Evidently not, since there was no municipal court and she hadn't put one in herself. He'd need a weight room, too. He'd have to maintain his condition and without the exercise of ranch work, he'd have to develop a program. He hated jogging but he could swim, at least part of the year. Well, it would give him something to think about besides Yelisa.

And he promptly began to think of Yelisa. She'd kept her part of the bargain, she'd married him. He thought about that night at Dightman's when she'd blown up the condom. Poor old Mabel, she'd never be the same. How shocked everyone had been. And how little Yelisa had cared or even noticed. She did what she wanted and just seemed to assume that the rest of the world – what? – didn't count? No, that wasn't it. She wasn't so egotistical as to think that her opinion was the only one of value. And she wasn't so self-centered that she simply didn't consider that other people would have opinions. It was more like she'd decided to notice other people's opinions only when the people were directly affected by her actions or it was convenient to herself to notice them. It was much the same way he lived but he was surprised to find another person who shared the attitude. Especially a woman. It seemed to him that women were much more vulnerable to public opinion than men were. Maybe not.

Since she'd kept her part of the bargain, he would keep his, if possible. He thought sardonically that it would be too ironic to practice birth control rigorously all these years to find that he was sterile. The thought of fathering a child still scared him. What if he and Yelisa couldn't maintain their life together? What of the child then? God knew he'd seen enough broken homes and one-parent children. It hurt like hell to have one parent absent from a child's life. What if he found he was like grandparents were said to be – spoil the kid for a few hours and then leave or take it home when it got to be a nuisance? That would be a hell of a way for a father to feel toward his own children.

Children? Plural? Wesley shook his head. So his sub-conscious had already dealt with the issue. There would be children and he would be their father and would love and cherish them as he loved and cherished their mother. What if he couldn't? What if he found he was not able to accept the challenge and responsibility of fatherhood? He pulled the drapery open a little and looked out across the lake. Not Klamath Lake. Some funny name. There was a brochure on the table that told all about Klamath Falls. He picked it up and found the little super-simplified map. Lake Ewauna. Fed by the shortest river in the world. How about that?

It was fun to rig the equipment and test it. It took a long time, Jimmy tuning the keyboard, Barney setting up his traps, the others hooking up the amps and testing them, running to and fro between the control boards and the stage. The stage was portable and was set up in the rodeo arena, in front of the chutes. Tomorrow the rodeo would happen there but tonight the space was theirs. The grandstand wasn't real big but it was a hell of a lot bigger than the one at the Wheeler County Fairgrounds in Fossil. The dressing room was a trailer parked behind the stage and they took turns suiting up; there wasn't room for all of them at once. Suddenly, it was time. They were introduced to a couple of local deejays and chatted for a few minutes. Wesley wondered belatedly if adding himself to the bill and changing the name of the group was going to cause problems.

Monte explained the situation and one of the deejays went out front to introduce them. Then they were on. They ran onto the stage, took their places, and acknowledged the applause. The grandstand was about two-thirds full but the area between the stands and the stage was filled with fans. They opened with one of their early hits and the audience ate it up. After a few numbers, the people in the stands seemed to realize that Wesley was back and they missed the first part of each of the early songs by renewing their applause after they recognized it.

Wesley saw car lights approaching the stage across the race track. It was too far away for him to recognize Yelisa, even if it had been light, but he knew she was in the car. Then he saw tail lights going back across the field and a deputy sheriff moved to head Yelisa off as she and Vern Worsham approached the front of the stage. The crowd continued to applaud after Wesley and the boys had left the stage. They went back and did a two-song encore. The second time they left the stage, they piled into the van, collecting Yelisa and Vern as they went, and drove into town for dinner. They found a place with a liquor license although they were all so high with their reception that they really didn't need any more stimulation.

The dinner was good but not great. They signed a few autographs, mostly for people who weren't sure exactly who they were but, from their clothes and talk, deduced they must be the fellas from the show over to the fairgrounds. Barney gave Vern the key to his room; he and the others wouldn't need it. They'd be busy packing until time to leave for Angels Camp. Vern decided to come back and watch the second show. Yelisa was excited and happy for Wesley. This first gig outside Fossil was an impressive omen of good times to come.

The stands were packed to capacity for the second show and their reception was everything they could wish for. It even looked for a few minutes as if they might be mobbed. Not that they actually wanted to be mobbed, but it was exciting. They'd done their share of running from fans in the old days.

Wesley and Yelisa were finally alone together at the motel. Wesley was in a chair with his legs stretched out in front of him, watching Yelisa, who was the luggage rack, rummaging through her little suitcase.

"The house is a lot bigger than it used to be," she said. "I never noticed before that it echoes."

"You never noticed how lonely you were before."

"I'm not going to pander to your overweening conceit and tell you I missed you. Damn, I was sure I put them in."

"What are you looking for?"

"Pictures of me and my new plane."

"How are you getting along with your lessons? Lesson? You had one today, didn't you?"

"Yes. Here they are." She handed them to him and sat on the arm of his chair. "Isn't she a beauty?"

'They're both beauties. I'm glad it got here for today."

"I think I'm going to love flying."

'That's great. That'll mean a lot more time together." He kissed her and she kissed him. After a bit, he said, "Robbie called. There've been a couple of changes in our itinerary."

"For the better."

"For the better. After Angels Camp tomorrow, we go to L.A. for a recording date that Robbie's set up for us. Then we're going to Tucson. We'll be there two weeks before we play Casper. Robbie's trying to fill in some time between Casper and Red Rocks."

"I'll make the changes on my calendar. I can't make Angels Camp – I have to get back and work out a solution to that crumbling on level twelve. But I'll be at Red Rocks. I used to go there a lot when I was in college. It's not far from Golden, you know."

"Golden's where you went to school?"

"Yeah. I might make it to Tucson. Although I'm not sure even you're worth Arizona in the summer."

"Maybe I can convince you."

He settled her on his lap and kissed her throat, her face, the back of her neck. He brushed his lips over her ear lobe and into the V of her shirt.

Wesley went to Angels Camp that night and Yelisa flew back to Fossil the next morning. The summer passed quickly, each concert as successful as they could wish and the single recording gathering momentum up the charts. Wesley and Yelisa talked on the phone every day and spent a number of days and nights together, mostly one at a time. It wasn't until early fall that Yelisa gave Wesley what she hoped was good news.

He had been home for nearly a week, excited about the tour and the single, glad to be home to rest in the serenity of Yelisa's happiness. One beautiful, crisp September day, they went up into the mountains on a trail ride. The horses were as eager for the outing as the people. Homer kept them exercised but he didn't ride them. Jack went along, enjoying the company but intent on the exciting smells of the forest. The scattered tamaracks were brightly golden and glowed against the solemn green of the conifers.

Wesley and Yelisa wore light jackets in the cool shadows of the woods and, when they came to a little creek, they dismounted. They let the horses drink, and just dropped the reins, knowing that they wouldn't stray far. They walked along the bank of the creek, catching up on the trivia that makes up the fabric of life.

"Remember I told you it was going to be a problem to find a replacement for Tom?" Yelisa asked.

"Yeah."

"I moved Eldon Richards up. He's a good engineer and he's been married a couple of years. He's young but he's working out really well."

"What's his being married two years got to do with it?" Wesley asked curiously.

Yelisa grinned. "Unmarried men are often not very steady; they tend to flit from job to job. A man who has been married more than eight or ten years is often cheating on his wife, and the strain spills over into his work. Besides, if he'd cheat on his wife, what wouldn't he do to a comparative stranger?"

"It's a point of view, all right."

"As an employer, I'm totally pragmatic."

"Yeah. By the way, how young is Richards?"

Yelisa thought a few seconds. "He's about my age."

"You're old enough to run the operation but a man the same age may be too young to superintend part of it? I don't understand."

"It's a matter of experience, really. I was practically brought up on the premises. I spent every minute I could at the mine or the plant or in the office. Richards had never seen a mercury mine until he came to us four years ago."

"I see."

She changed the subject and spoke excitedly. "Your song is at number six this week."

"Yeah."

"Are you happy, Wesley?" She thought she knew the answer but he so seldom smiled or laughed that she couldn't be completely sure. And she needed to know.

He looked down at her and a look of deep, satisfied contentment, tinged with excitement, spread across his face. "I have nearly everything I ever wanted – my wife and my work."

Yelisa searched his face. "What's included in nearly?"

"Children."

"The old fear is gone?" Yelisa could hardly contain her joy for another minute.

"Gone. Today I feel like God must have felt on about the fourth day."

"Make it the fifth day," she said, laughing happily.

"We made a baby."

"It's due about the end of April."

Wesley put his hand on her belly and looked at her tenderly.

Chapter 13

The days passed in a happy swirl of work and preparation. Wesley spent several weeks, at intervals, on the road. And he and the boys had a couple of TV dates to appear on other people's programs and specials. Wesley didn't care too much for the TV dates, he preferred live audiences where he got the response at once.

Yelisa prepared the room across the hall from the sitting room as a nursery. She made a trip to Portland to buy furniture for it and new curtains. She put down a couple of big rugs but decided against a carpet because it couldn't be taken up and washed if necessary. Agnes was in a delighted tizzy most of the time, thinking of details that would have escaped Yelisa.

It was a happy time although Wesley and Yelisa missed each other terribly when they were apart. Yelisa thought philosophically that it might strengthen their bond, it was certain that they weren't going to have a chance to get tired of one another. She would be glad when Wesley got back from this last trip and would be home for most of the rest of the winter.

Wesley had been gone for Thanksgiving and Helen, mercifully, went to Stuart's family. Yelisa and Agnes had quite a happy little celebration but Yelisa couldn't help being a little blue. Her pregnancy had begun to show a few days earlier and she wanted Wesley's warmth beside her. She played his new album almost incessantly and Agnes was thankful it was cheerful because the baby would certainly have acquired a melancholy disposition otherwise.

Yelisa was at the office one day in early December, looking forward to seeing Wesley the next day. It felt like years since she'd had him with her. Luckily there wasn't much of importance for her to see to at the office because her mind was not on her work for once. She was doing her best to concentrate when the phone rang. She picked it up and looked out the window at the light covering of snow. She hoped the roads wouldn't be icy for Wesley tomorrow.

"Okay, put her on, Faye...Mrs. Britton?...Oh...Oh, I see....I don't know...I suppose I'd better...No, don't do that....I'll drive right over. Wait at your place for me, will you?...Okay....Yes, in a few minutes."

Yelisa put the receiver down, took her coat off the rack and stopped to tell Faye that she wouldn't be back that afternoon. As she drove into town, she thought over what Mrs. Britton had told her. She had made a decision but it was necessarily subject to revision. She pulled up in front of the trailer that was the manager's home and office in the park where Trudy lived.

Mrs. Britton answered the door holding a tiny baby wrapped in a dirty towel. Yelisa declined her invitation to sit down and the two women stood in the middle of the living room while Mrs. Britton said all over again what she'd already said on the phone. The baby was making soft whimpering sounds.

"The baby was born two weeks ago. Trudy, she never cared anything about it. She run off with that Tom Plank last night. I went over to her trailer to see what needed to be done before I could rent it again and, lo and behold, there's the baby just layin' on the floor, wrapped in this towel. Well, I didn't know what to do. First I thought of callin' the sheriff but then I thought, what's the use of that? Mark Leslie wouldn't know what to do any more'n I do. Then I thought of you. Since you'd been payin' the rent and givin' the girl money, I figured maybe you'd be the one to call."

Yelisa took the baby and unwrapped it, quickly wrapping it again. "I'll take her with me. Do you have something warm to put around her?"

"I don't know as I do. You could take that old crocheted shawl, I guess. If you'll have it washed and bring it back."

"Yes, all right. Get it, would you, please?"

Yelisa put the baby on the floor of the Mercedes and drove over to the drug store. She didn't like to leave the child alone but she didn't want to take her in the store, either. The baby was still weakly trying to cry and Yelisa picked her up and honked until Eloise Fairbanks, who was the clerk and the owner, came out. She explained her plight and Eloise hurried to get some bottles of pre-mixed formula and a box of disposable diapers. She was all agog over the baby but Yelisa didn't waste much time in explanations. There would be about a hundred versions of it all over town by evening, she knew. Well, let them have their fun.

She got home as quickly as she could and grabbed one of the bottles of formula and hurried inside with the baby.

"Aggie," she called as she went through the back door. "Aggie, come and see what I've got."

Aggie popped up from the range, where she had been peering into the oven, checking on a batch of cookies she was baking for Wesley's homecoming the next day.

"Something good, I hope," Aggie said. Then she saw the bundle in Yelisa's arms and her mouth dropped open.

"The best. A brand new baby."

"Now, where in the name of goodness, did you get a baby? I swear, it isn't safe to let you out of the house these days."

"She's hungry, Aggie. We need to heat this formula and get it into her."

"A girl, huh? Room temperature's okay. Here, let me have her, I'll feed her."

"Nothing doing, she's mine. I found her. Well, sort of. Come into the living room and I'll tell you about it while I feed her."

Aggie fixed the bottle and Yelisa sat down in a rocking chair and cuddled the baby while she fed her. As the baby sucked desperately, Yelisa told Aggie the story.

"Well, it's a shame," Aggie pronounced. "A damn shame."

"It is that," Yelisa agreed. She put the baby across her lap on her tummy and gently rubbed her back, waiting for her to burp. But the baby merely went to sleep. "I got some diapers and some more formula from Eloise Fairbanks, but we need a lot more stuff, Aggie. Will you bring the diapers inside and then go back into town and get some things while I bathe the baby?"

"Sure. Poor little mite. She's filthy."

"I don't think she's been bathed since she was born. Just rolled up in this dirty old towel."

Aggie shook her head in wonder as she went out to the car for the diapers. She returned to find Yelisa upstairs running a basin full of warm water.

"I've been thinking what we need." Yelisa rattled off a list of supplies as she bathed the baby.

"Wait a minute," Aggie protested, "not so fast. I don't take shorthand like Faye does."

'Sorry," Yelisa said. And then came to her senses. "Well, for heaven's sake, you raised two sons, you know what we need better than I do. Go into town and get it, will you?"

"Of course. It'll take me a little while."

"Okay. I don't approve of disposable diapers but this is an emergency. It's a good thing I had so much spare time while Wesley was away. At least the nursery's habitable, even if we don't have any clothes ready."

"I'll be back as quick as I can," Agnes said as she left the room. She let Jack in as she left and he trotted upstairs to sniff anxiously at the baby.

"It's a baby, Jack," Yelisa told him. "I don't know if she's ours or not, but you'd better get used to the idea of at least one around."

Jack wagged his tail and whined. Yelisa dried the baby and applied a diaper. She wrapped her in a receiving blanket and carried her into the sitting room. She sat in a corner of the sofa and cuddled the baby who was gazing at her solemnly. Jack sat at her feet and watched them both, uncertain as to the meaning of this arrival. Yelisa smiled at the baby who suddenly gave her a big smile in return. She was overcome by a burst of maternal love and began to speak in such shameless baby-talk that Jack was embarrassed for her.

The sound of a car driving under the porte-cochere annoyed her and she waited impatiently for the doorbell to ring so whoever it was would get tired of waiting and go away. Instead, after

176

the sound of a car door slamming, someone stamped snow off on the porch and the front door opened. A minute later Wesley came in and Yelisa stood up. He stopped in the middle of the room and stared at her.

"But it's only December!" he exclaimed in total bewilderment.

Yelisa grinned and turned sideways, holding the baby up a little.

"What the hell have you done now?" he demanded, almost angrily. "How did even you manage whatever it is you did manage?"

"We didn't expect you until tomorrow. How'd the concert go? Are you cold? Do you want a drink or a cup of tea?"

He shrugged off his coat and tossed it onto a chair. "I swear to God, you'd make a man take to drink. Where did you get that child?"

"It's Trudy's. She and Tom Plank took off last night and left this tiny little girl all alone on the floor of that cold trailer house."

"They called you? Who called you?"

"The landlady. I couldn't leave her there, Wesley. That old biddy didn't want her. And I couldn't just let the authorities take her. Poor little devil."

The baby whimpered and Yelisa looked down at her and told her that everything was all right, patting her softly. Jack whined and looked worried. Wesley rolled his eyes and guided Yelisa to the sofa. She sat down and he sat beside her. Jack sat in front of them, watching them anxiously.

"Why not?" Wesley asked reasonably.

"Why not?" Yelisa was absorbed in the baby. "Oh, the authorities. We'll have to check with the lawyer but I think she can't be adopted since her mother is alive but unavailable to sign the papers. That means foster homes. Which may or may not be okay."

"And you're a hard-headed businesswoman. If you think we ought to take her because she might be mine, don't. Because it's flat impossible that she's mine. Trudy was pregnant when I met her."

"It isn't that, Wesley. It's the baby herself. I know we can't take every unfortunate child we see and it's easy not to as long as they're at a distance. But this little one was given to us. It just seems meant, somehow." She searched his face for a long moment. "Shall we keep her? If we do, you'll probably have to swear she's yours."

Wesley looked from Yelisa to the baby and back at Yelisa. All the repressed paternity of the last twenty years welled up inside him. "We'll keep her. Let me have her."

Yelisa gave him the baby and watched him curiously. He held her in the crook of his arm and patted her little rump reassuringly. He talked to her, softly and gently, and Jack relaxed and lay with his chin on his crossed paws.

"You handle her as if you'd raised a dozen babies. How come you're so handy with them?"

"Twin sisters."

Yelisa was reminded that he had taken some time to visit his family. "How is everyone? Did you have a good visit?"

"Great. I invited 'em here for Christmas."

Yelisa laughed. "All of 'em? In three weeks all my in-laws will be here?"

"Don't worry about it. They're all real happy about you. They think you're good for me."

Yelisa remembered something else. "Oh, Wesley, the new single is at nine and the album is seven."

"Yeah. Right after we went gold on the first one. The boys are pretty happy about it. The company executives are pretty happy about it, too."

"Have you started to put together the next album?"

"Not really. Some ideas are floating around. It's a good thing we've got the rest of the winter to prepare."

"A half-dozen personal appearances and that charity thing in Philadelphia. Other than that, you've got the whole winter to devote to your rapidly-growing family. Will we have room for everyone who's coming?"

"How many bedrooms are there?"

"Not counting the service wing, seven. There used to be nine but I knocked two of them together for my sitting room."

"We only need four if everyone comes and I think Denny and Sylvia are going to her family. And if the girls bring boyfriends, we'll still have room."

Yelisa was surprised. "Boyfriends? How old are your sisters?"

"Twenty. They're both juniors at Arizona State."

"Let me have her now." Wesley handed the sleeping baby over and Yelisa held her so she could watch her face and let her curl one tiny hand around her finger. "Twenty?" She did some calculations in her head. "You were nearly grown up when they were born."

"Well, there was a little family mix-up just at first. Mom and Dad got carried away and Mom was not quite sixteen when I was born. Dad's family yanked him out of town and he thought she'd given me up for adoption. But Mom's pretty stubborn. She and Dad were finally married when I was four. My brother Denny was born seven years later. The twins were kind of an embarrassing accident, I gather. At least, the folks used to think so. Now they just laugh about it."

"Does Denny have children?"

"Two little boys. Jerry and Lenny."

"Twins?"

"Yeah."

"But, Wesley, I don't want twins," Yelisa said anxiously.

"You shouldn't have popped that condom. I knew you'd be sorry some day."

"I'll never be sorry for that. Besides, now that I think about it, twins wouldn't be much harder to manage than just one. Are they?"

"Not the way we're going to do it. I suppose Aggie'll stay on, even through twins?"

"It would take a lot more than twins to dislodge Aggie. She's really part of the family. She just gets stuck with all the disagreeable chores."

"There you are. We'll hire a nurse for the children and let her do the hard stuff. You and I will just kick back and enjoy them."

Yelisa smiled. "Aggie's way ahead of you. She wants to be the nurse and let someone else take over the cooking and housework."

"Excellent. Listen, as long as the baby's sleeping, let's put her down. Give her here."

Wesley took the baby and they went into the nursery. He put her in the crib and Yelisa smoothed a light blanket over her. Yelisa linked her arm in his and they stood looking at her.

"What shall we name her?" Yelisa asked.

"Camille."

"Camille Callaghan? Camille Callaghan. Does it sound all right?"

Wesley nodded and led her out of the nursery and across the hall to the sitting room. They sat on the sofa and Wesley turned her so she lay across his lap with her head on his shoulder.

"Put your feet up," he said. Yelisa obeyed and Wesley put his hand on her abdomen. "One or two, or even three – it'll be all right." He looked down at her seriously. "You know that Trudy may show up sometime to claim Camille."

"I suppose so. But we'll deal with it if it comes." She laughed. "Won't your folks be amazed when they get here? Grandparents again and another one due in April. It's going to sound very funny to people. I mean, siblings about the same age but obviously not twins."

"Let 'em puzzle over it. Mom and Dad will take it in stride. And Julie and Sara'll want to play with her all the time."

Yelisa put her hands on his cheeks and kissed his lips.

Chapter 14

Two weeks before Christmas, Yelisa was sitting at her desk reading a report and making notes on a pad. It was quitting time and a lot of the men were leaving the wash house to go for their cars and pickups in the parking lot. There was still some snow on the ground. Yelisa was absorbed in her work and had lost track of time until a horribly ominous rumbling sound brought her to a sharp awareness of the world around her. She glanced at her watch and saw that the time was right for the charges in the mine to go off. But the blast was too loud, the ground shook too hard. She jerked to her feet and ran outside into a huge dust cloud that was rising from the mouth of the shaft.

The men stopped in their tracks and stared with horror at the headrig for a moment. Then they began to mill around, some running toward the office, others toward the mine. Yelisa grabbed a miner by the arm and he stopped.

"Go into the office," she said. "Call John Courtland and Doc Hutchinson. Get the ambulance from Condon. And get some masks and respirators."

The miner nodded. "Right, Mrs. Callaghan."

Before he was finished speaking, Yelisa was gone. She ran into the elevator shack at the headrig. Emmett, the elevator operator, turned to her. She stepped into the elevator and Emmett grabbed her by the arm.

"Let me alone, Emmett, some of my men are down there."

"Mrs. Callaghan! No! You don't know how bad it is."

"Let go, Emmett." She pried his hand off her arm. "Lower the cage. They may be trapped down there. Get someone to organize a crew and have them wait until I tell you to send them down."

"I can't let you do it," Emmett said desperately.

Yelisa pushed him away from the elevator lever and pulled down. The cage started to descend slowly and she jumped into it. Emmett hesitated with his hand hovering over the lever but decided to obey her. He looked around for someone to give Yelisa's order to.

"Will! Come here," he said.

"Yeah? What can I do, Emmett?"

"Yelisa's down there. She wants you to get some men ready to dig the guys down there out when she gives the word. Get a crew together."

Will was horrified. "What the hell did you let her go down there for?"

"I know, there'll be hell to pay but I couldn't stop her. Get going, will you?"

Will ran toward a group of miners and began to wave his arms and shout. The men gathered around him and couple had to be restrained from going into the mine when he told them Yelisa had gone down. She had a special relationship with her men; they respected her and liked her and felt protective of her. She was fair and treated them with dignity and warmth. They were aware of her affection for them and returned it in full measure. They were also very interested in her condition, and fully knowledgeable of the danger of mercury poisoning that she was running by going into the mine.

The cage rose to the top of the shaft and a couple of miners, Oshen and Harrington, stepped out, coughing and choking. Some of the men led them out into the yard and it took a moment or two for them to get their breath so they could talk.

Harrington recovered first. "Yelisa's down there. She sent us to tell you to go on down. Merryman and Landford and some other guys are still down there."

"She said to take a count and find out who's here so we'll know who's down there," Oshen added.

Eldon Richards ran up to them. "Who's still down there? Where's Yelisa?"

"She's down there," Will answered. "We don't know who else is still…"

Will was interrupted by another rumble that sent another, smaller cloud of dust rising from the shaft. There was a cry of dismay from the men. They had to wait until the dust settled somewhat before a relief party could go down.

Inside the mine, Yelisa was lying half buried by the rubble of the explosion. The only light was from a battery-operated lantern but Yelisa could see several miners among the broken and fallen timbers and rocks. Everyone was coughing and some of the men were groaning. Yelisa pushed the ore off her as far as she could reach but when she tried to sit up, she fell back in pain, protecting her left side. Her legs and pelvis remained covered in rubble. She put a fold of her smock over her mouth and nose, doing the only thing that she could to protect her child from the mercury.

Landford was the first one up. He was bruised and shaken but not really hurt. He stood up and listened intently for a moment. "The elevator's coming down."

"Good," Yelisa said. "Landford, see if there's anything you can do for the others."

Landford went from one to another of the miners, checking their injuries as best he could. Some could sit up, others couldn't. Only one of them, Carson, was able to stand. He got to his feet and assisted Landford. After they had done what little they could, Landford came to Yelisa.

"What about you, Mrs. Callaghan? Are you okay?"

"Not quite. I think my leg's broken."

"Hey, Carson," Landford called, "come over here and help me."

Carson came over and they began to gently pull the rubble away from Yelisa.

Carson stopped and froze. "Oh, my God!"

Landford stopped work to look and Yelisa tried to sit up. She saw that Carson had uncovered a miner's knee before she fell back. The body was evidently under her with a layer of rubble between them.

"Help me move her," Landford said.

They lifted her as gently as they could but a small cry of pain escaped her. They hesitated.

"Keep going, boys," she urged. "Hurry and get him out."

She bit her lip to keep from crying out as they shifted her a few feet away. She watched tensely as they uncovered the body. It was Merryman. Carson tried to revive him but his chest was completely crushed. Yelisa watched sadly.

"It's no use," Carson said. "He's gone."

"Poor devil," Landford said. "I wonder what went wrong."

Landford put his shirt over Merryman's face.

"We'll be able to tell when we get this all cleared away," Yelisa said.

"I wonder how long it'll take 'em to get us out," Landford said.

"Maybe we'll get lucky and it won't take long," Carson said hopefully.

Yelisa wanted to keep the men's minds off the fact that they were trapped underground. So far they'd been good but you never could tell when someone would panic. She herself was so tightly strung up, although being underground didn't ordinarily bother her, that she felt she might panic if she didn't keep a very tight rein on herself.

"Carson, see if you can figure out exactly who was down here," she said. "There may be someone else buried."

"Okay," he answered and moved to a couple of miners to ask questions.

"Landford, see if you can find a water jug," she ordered. "We need to wash this dust out of our throats. And put your undershirts over your noses and mouths," she said loud enough for everyone to hear. "We've got to keep as much mercury dust and vapor out as possible."

Yelisa set the example by replacing the fold of her smock over her nose and mouth. Landford tied his t-shirt over his face and went to help the others who couldn't manage by themselves.

Wesley was in the sitting room that afternoon. He'd been working at the piano downstairs but he'd begun to feel stale and tired so he went upstairs and, while Agnes was busy in the kitchen, picked Camille up. He was sitting in an easy chair with the baby on his lap, watching her wave her hands and coo happily when he heard Agnes coming up the stairs. He was enjoying the baby very much but he knew Agnes didn't approve of him picking her up just because she was awake. He braced himself to face out her disapproval when something in the sound of her steps made him uneasy. They were too quick, too staccato. He turned his head as she came into the room and saw that she was crying quietly and was very upset. He knew there was some kind of bad news. He stood, cradling Camille in one arm, holding his other hand out to Agnes.

"Aggie? What is it?"

"There's been an accident," she said, trying to stifle her tears.

"Yelisa?" He didn't wait for his dread to take shape, he was filled with a formless fear. Something had happened to Yelisa.

"I don't know," Agnes said. "Faye said there was a premature detonation in the mine. Some of the men were still down there. Yelisa went down."

Wesley nodded. Of course she went down. That was her job.

Agnes continued. "And there was another blast."

Wesley couldn't speak. His mind shrieked the word no over and over. He had no coherent thoughts or feelings, just the denial that anything bad could have happened to Yelisa. He handed Camille to Agnes and ran out of the room to his pickup, not even stopping for a coat.

When he skidded the pickup to a stop in the mine yard, his mind was still saying no again and again. He ran to the elevator shack. Emmett was there, looking very pale and strained.

"Where is she?" Wesley demanded, hoping that Agnes' information was wrong but knowing it was a forlorn hope.

"Down below," Emmett answered.

Wesley got into the cage. "Take it down."

Emmett lowered the elevator and Wesley stepped out. It took him a moment to orient himself. Richards was directing the work of digging through the blockage and Wesley went to him. One of the miners handed him a mask as he went by and Wesley put it on absently.

"What's the situation, Eldon?" he asked.

Richards felt a pang of profound compassion for Wesley. It must be an awful thing to have a wife who constantly ran the risks Yelisa did. He was thankful that his own wife stayed at home and tended to their children and the house like she was supposed to.

"We don't know, Wesley," he said. "Yelisa's in there. Some of them are still alive, we can hear them shout now and then. But we don't know how many there are or how many are hurt."

"How can I help?" Wesley asked.

190

Richards shook his head. "Not much we can do until we get a hole cleared."

They could hear the sirens of the ambulance and E.M.T. truck. The sound got louder and louder until it abruptly stopped near the mouth of the shaft.

"There's the ambulance," Wesley said unnecessarily. "Is the doctor here yet?"

"I don't know."

"Send one of the men up and see. I'll take over for him."

Richards nodded. "Will. Come over here."

Will turned to see what the superintendent wanted.

'Go see if Doc Hutchinson is here yet," Richards said. "If he is, ask him to wait on the surface until I send for him. John Courtland, too."

Will didn't want to go up, he wanted to stay and help get the boss out. It was better to be doing something than standing around up there, wondering about everything.

"Can't you send..."

Wesley interrupted him by taking his shovel from him. "I'll take over for you," he said. Will looked at him and Wesley nodded once, his eyes dark with pain and fear. "I need to," he added.

Will reluctantly acknowledged a better claim than his own. "Okay."

Wesley began to dig and Will went up to the surface.

Landford was shouting, trying to let the rescue party know that they were still alive when Yelisa raised her hand for silence.

"Listen," she said.

Everyone stopped talking and moving. They could hear the sound of the miners digging on the other side of the wall. Voices came to them indistinctly.

"They're already digging," Landford breathed.

"I wish we knew how bad the fall is," Carson said.

"It can't be too bad since we can hear them already," Yelisa said cheerfully.

They all listened intently. Yelisa looked around as one of the men groaned softly. She noticed that another man was lying terribly still. She could see part of the rock fall and as she watched, a faint shaft of light pierced it.

A muffled voice came to them, "We're through!"

Then Wesley's voice; they could feel his urgency even through the wall of rocks. "Hurry. Someone go up and bring Doc and Courtland down."

The miners around Yelisa gave a cheer and a couple of minutes later Wesley made his way through the opening at the top of the fall. He looked around and saw Yelisa near Merryman's corpse. He went to her and hunkered down, placing his body so it hid Merryman from her.

Richards came down the wall and went to Carson, seeing that Wesley was with Yelisa. The miners from the other side came in, some to finish the opening so they could begin to take the men out; some to bring stretchers and blankets and masks.

Wesley knelt beside Yelisa and said her name. She smiled up at him through her pain. He put his mask over her nose and mouth.

"Hi, cowboy," she said.

Wesley turned to call the doctor over. Yelisa put her hand on his arm. "Don't call him, Wesley. It's only a broken leg and maybe a rib or two. Same as you and old Prairie Schooner."

Wesley looked at her and understood that she wanted her men taken care of first but he was unable to refrain from asking the doctor to see to his wife first.

"Over here, Doc," he called.

Dr. Hutchinson crunched over the chunks of ore to Yelisa. She smiled at him and Wesley but her voice was commanding.

"See to the men first, Doc."

"Not until I've checked you over."

"If I get very upset and hysterical, will it make things worse for me?" she asked, knowing quite well that in cases of mercury poisoning, quiet and calmness were among the first things the doctor demanded.

"It won't do you any good in all this mercury," the doctor answered. He handed

Wesley a mask. He'd been the official mine doctor for forty years and more and prided himself on keeping up with the latest treatments. He also knew Yelisa very well and believed what she said.

"Then you'd better see to the men. I'll still be here when you're finished."

Wesley knew there were things between the doctor and Yelisa that they weren't saying. He didn't know what but he knew that Yelisa needed help.

"Yelisa, let the doctor examine you."

Her face broke out into a cold sweat. She was terribly afraid for the baby she carried but the discipline of years held. Her men must be taken care of before she could seek care for herself. No matter what the risk. "The sooner my men are taken care of, the sooner I'll be taken care of." She knew Wesley wouldn't understand the depth of her feelings in the matter and she didn't know if he – or if she – could forgive her if anything happened to the child because of her refusal. She tightened her fingers on his hand. "Please, Wesley."

Wesley nodded reluctantly and the doctor went to one of the miners. Wesley stayed beside Yelisa. He could see she was in pain, both physical and mental. He didn't know if he could ease either kind of pain.

"You've got guts, kid," he said.

"Put the mask on, Wesley," she ordered.

He shook his head.

Yelisa spoke peremptorily. "Do it. You don't know how mercury poisoning affects people. As soon as we get out of here, promise me you'll shower and change your clothes. Boots, too."

"All right," he said, putting the mask on, humoring her. "Easy, now."

"Yes, I mustn't get excited. The heat makes it worse and so does excitement. See, the mercury enters through the nose and mouth and sweat glands, mostly. But it'll wash off and sweating helps get rid of it. I don't know how it'll affect the baby."

Wesley didn't know either and her fear was very contagious. But he made himself speak calmly and evenly. They could always make other babies, however greatly they would grieve if they lost this one. But there was only one Yelisa. She must be protected whatever the cost.

"It's okay," he said. "It's going to be all right."

Yelisa looked into his eyes, tears welling up in hers. "Not for Merryman. Oh, Wesley, Merryman's dead."

"Shhh. You couldn't have prevented it. It isn't your fault."

"Yes, it is. I knew he was getting careless with his charges. I should have fired him."

"That's hindsight, Yelisa. Accidents happen. If you'd fired him, someone else would have hired him. Maybe there'd have been a worse accident with more people killed."

"Maybe." She used the tail of her smock to dry her eyes. "Thanks, Wesley. But it won't make it any easier for his wife. Widow. Or his kids."

"I know." Wesley could well imagine what Mrs. Merryman would feel, what the children would feel. "I know."

Will came to talk to Yelisa for a moment. He told her that the miners and plant workers were all outside, worried about her. As they were talking, the last man was evacuated and Landford brought a stretcher over. Dr. Hutchinson examined her, palpating her abdomen, and shook his head when she cried out as he pressed on her left side.

"All right," he said, "bring the stretcher here, boys."

They put the stretcher beside her and carefully lifted her onto it. She kept her lips tightly together so she wouldn't make any more sounds. Wesley and the others carried the stretcher to the elevator and signaled for it to be taken up. It was dark on the surface but the yard lights were on and Yelisa could see that the men were still there waiting to see how she was. She knew they'd been told about Merryman and Will had told her that they were blaming the powder man for the accident and were very anxious about her. Richards came to her but the others remained at a respectful distance, watching intently.

"Did you get that count, Eldon?" Yelisa wanted to know.

"Yes. Everyone's accounted for."

"That's a relief," she said. "I don't know how long I'll be laid up. Keep the plant running as long as you have ore. We should be able to re-open the mine as soon as the state safety…"

Wesley interrupted her. "Later, Yelisa. Eldon can handle things for a couple of days."

Yelisa grinned at him. "Okay. Tilt the stretcher so I can see my guys."

Wesley scowled at her. "Yelisa, the quicker we get you to a hospital, the better it's going to be."

Yelisa spoke imperiously. "Tilt the stretcher." Then she remembered that husbands required different handling than employees. She smiled at him guiltily. "Please?"

Wesley glanced at the doctor, who nodded. They rested the end of the stretcher on the ground and held the other end up enough so the men could see her. She held onto Wesley's arm with one hand and raised the other to give Churchill's victory sign, grinning at the men. A great cheer went up and Wesley marveled at his wife as they put her in the ambulance. He and Dr. Hutchinson got into the vehicle with her and Wesley held her hand as they sped toward the clinic. The doctor gave her some water and held the kidney pan for her to spit it out. She seemed to know the drill – she forced some water through her nose without choking. When the doctor started to sponge her face and hands with a wet towel, Wesley took it from him and washed the mercury dust off her.

She was so slight. How was it possible that she commanded the respect and affection of all those men? How did she do it? By caring, Wesley thought. By running the same risks they did and caring about them. They knew it wasn't just a public relations act, they knew that she really did care. Her grief at Merryman's death was real and they understood that. He admired her courage and hoped that he would be able to behave similarly in similar circumstances but he was afraid that the price of her courage might be very high. If the baby was lost or injured...He couldn't complete the thought, even in his own mind. But he was determined that she wouldn't suffer more than she had to, no matter what happened next. He would shield her to the best of his ability but, he reflected bleakly, that ability didn't extend very far in this case.

Chapter 15

The doctor and Yelisa disappeared when they got to the clinic and the nurses wouldn't let him see her. He went to the phone and called Agnes. He explained the situation and asked her to come and bring some clean clothes and boots for him. When she got there, he demanded a shower and one of the orderlies took him down a bare hall to a cubbyhole of a shower stall. Afterwards he went back to the waiting room to worry with Agnes. She was trying to be good; she sat very still, watching the door for the doctor. Wesley went to the window and stood looking out into the darkness, trying to believe that everything would be all right.

Dr. Hutchinson came into the room and nodded at Agnes. He went to Wesley and put his hand on Wesley's shoulder. "She's going to be all right, son," he said.

Agnes relaxed against the chair back and Wesley sighed deeply.

"How bad is it?" he asked. "Are we going to lose the baby?"

"Yelisa's a good strong, healthy woman. I've seen pregnancies brought to term even after injuries worse than these. There are fractures of the left tibia and fibula, the spleen is probably fractured, and the left kidney is bruised. Nearly her whole left side is bruised. She must have been thrown against the rock face by the blast."

"What does it mean?" Wesley asked, frowning. "How serious is a fractured spleen?"

"We'll watch it closely tonight and we should know for sure tomorrow morning whether it's fractured or not. If it is, it'll probably have to come out. The damage to the kidney isn't bad. At least I don't think so. We'll watch it, too, of course. If we have to take the spleen, it'll increase the risk that she'll lose the baby. So I would recommend taking her to Portland if we have to operate."

"Yelisa mentioned mercury poisoning," Wesley said. "Is she affected?"

"Mercury's funny stuff," the doctor said. "She's not experiencing any symptoms yet and we're doing everything we can to eliminate any mercury from her system. We'll keep a close check and see what shows."

"Okay." Wesley nodded. "You know what you're doing. Whatever you say, Doc."

Dr. Hutchinson spoke wryly. "If I know Yelisa, and I do, it'll be whatever she says."

Wesley grinned and nodded. "Yeah. Can I see her now?"

"Her leg's been set and we put a cast on it. I thought it best not to tell her the risk to the baby.

We don't want her to get excited." He pointed to the hall. "Second door on the right."

There was an I.V. in Yelisa's arm and it was tied down so she couldn't disturb the needle. She was lying very still, watching the door. Whatever the doctor thought, she knew mercury and she knew there was some risk to the baby she was carrying. She didn't know how much the doctor would have told Wesley but she didn't want to worry him. Time enough to feel the pain if it happened. The door opened and Wesley and Agnes came into the room. She smiled at them. Wesley took her hand and looked down at her unsmilingly. Agnes stood beside him.

"I left Rita Samuels with Camille," Agnes said, "but I want to get back to feed her. So I'm going now unless you need me here, Yelisa."

"Thanks, Aggie. That reassures me more than anything could. Thank goodness Helen's in Europe and we don't have to cope with her on top of everything else. You go ahead, now. I'll be home in a day or two."

"Don't worry about the baby," Agnes said, "just rest and get well."

Agnes patted her hand and Wesley patted Agnes' shoulder. She smiled at them both and left the room.

Wesley was grateful to Agnes for setting her own feelings aside and leaving. He knew that Yelisa figured Agnes would not have gone if there was any danger to her or the baby so her going was practically a guarantee to Yelisa that everything was going to be okay. He knew how hard it was for Agnes to go, leaving Yelisa when everything was so uncertain. He resolved that he would call her often and report every development, no matter how small.

Yelisa moved restlessly. "I'm afraid I've damaged your wife, Wesley. But your baby's okay."

"Yeah. Thank God for that. But the damage to you is pretty comprehensive."

She put her hand on her left side, just under her ribs. "There's probably going to be a scar here." She looked at him anxiously. "Does it bother you?"

Wesley blinked. "Bother me? Of course it bothers me. Did you think I'd be indifferent?"

"I'd sort of hoped you wouldn't mind too much."

"You get yourself blown up and damn near killed and you hope I won't mind?"

"I mean about the scar."

Wesley shook his head as if to clear it. "The scar. The hell with the scar. It'll remind me how precious you are."

"Oh, Wesley." Tears welled up in her eyes and spilled over on her cheeks.

Wesley watched her helplessly. He wanted so much to protect her and there was just nothing he could do. She'd have to work through it herself, the pain was there for her to assimilate and he couldn't bear it for her. He took a tissue and blotted the tears from her cheeks."

"It's all right, Yelisa," he said meaninglessly. "It's okay now."

Yelisa took the tissue from him and wiped her eyes. "Doc says the others will be okay," she said tremulously. "Just broken bones and a concussion but nothing to panic about. Poor Merryman is our only tragedy."

"I know. I'll go see his family tomorrow."

"Would you?" I've been kind of worrying about that. Someone should and it'll be better for one of the family to go than to send Eldon."

"I figured." He touched her hair and the curve of her chin. "Go to sleep, now."

He turned out all the lights except one dimly-burning bulb by the sink. He drew a chair up beside her and sat down, taking her hand in his again.

"You need some sleep, too," she said. "Why don't you go on home? I'll be okay."

"Go to sleep."

"You're a stubborn man, Wesley Callaghan."

Wesley nodded and Yelisa smiled faintly as she closed her eyes. He sat there all night, leaving her side only for short turns up and down the corridor when the chair got too hard or he couldn't sit quietly any longer. She seemed to rest easier when he was there, sensing his presence even in her sleep. The nurse looked in periodically on mysterious errands. She smiled reassuringly at Wesley and brought him coffee a couple of times. Not having anything else to do, he drank it.

They chased him out early the next morning. Doc said there were tests to run and sent him to get some breakfast. Wesley went reluctantly and walked a few blocks to the café. He ordered a glass of orange juice and a cheese omelet. He was surprised to find that the omelet was not just scrambled eggs with melted cheese. It was probably delicious but, although he ate most of it, he didn't really taste it at all. He went back to the clinic and fell asleep on the sofa in the waiting room. Dr. Hutchinson woke him up a little before noon. Wesley sat up, damp from his contact with the plastic upholstery.

"There was blood in the needle, which means that her spleen is bleeding into her belly," the doctor explained. "It's going to have to come out, Wesley. But there's only a trace of mercury in the urine so I don't think we have anything to worry about in that respect. She's adamant about not going to Portland – can you change her mind?"

Wesley rubbed his temples. "Can you do the operation here?"

"Yes. I'd rather take her to Portland but we can do it here if we have to."

"I suppose I could badger her into changing her mind, but I rather not unless you think it might make the difference between saving her life and losing it."

"It might make the difference in saving the child, Wesley."

Wesley nodded. "That's the only lever I can see that we have. And I don't want to use it. If we lose this baby, she's going to blame herself no matter what she decided about the operation. I don't want anything I say to make it worse for her. Unless taking her to Portland will guarantee that we won't lose the baby?"

"I see your point. I don't agree with you but I understand. No, of course there's no guarantee. I'll make arrangements to operate this afternoon. I'll have to get Dr. Castlebury to come over from Heppner to assist."

Wesley called Agnes and persuaded her to stay with Camille. She might as well stay busy, there was nothing to do at the clinic but wait. Wait and worry. The operation was over about four that afternoon and they let Wesley sit with Yelisa in the recovery room. The nurses kept a frequent eye on her and Wesley sat with his forearms on the bedrail, resting his head on his hands. They had hooked up another IV and her hand was tied to the rail again. Yelisa's eyes fluttered open and she smiled fleetingly at him.

"The baby?" she asked in a small voice.

"The baby's okay. Doc Hutchinson says we're not going to lose him."

"You're not just saying that to keep me quiet?"

"No, it's true. The baby's safe if you mind the doctor."

She nodded and fell asleep. Wesley was still there, holding her hand through the rail when she stirred again a few hours later. She frowned and her eyes opened. She looked at Wesley and smiled.

"We didn't lose the baby?" she wanted to know.

"The baby's okay." He put his hand on her belly very lightly. "You did just fine."

"I thought maybe I'd dreamed you said he was okay."

"It wasn't a dream. They took out your spleen and had a look at your kidney and now everything's jake."

"Have you been here all this time?"

"It hasn't been so long."

"Camille's okay?"

"She's great. Aggie says she's going to smuggle her up here in a couple of days."

"Tell her not to bother. I'm going home tomorrow."

"All right."

"You don't believe me; you're humoring me. But I am."

"Oh, I believe you," he said. "There's only one thing – you aren't supposed to get up by yourself for a couple of days and you're to use a wheelchair for two or three weeks."

Yelisa started to laugh and stopped abruptly, surprised at the pain it caused. "A wheelchair? Me? Oh, no."

"For once you're going to have to do as you're told. The safety of the baby depends on it. Remember I told you he'd be okay as long as you mind the doctor?"

"You've got me this time," she said.

Wesley put his hand on her cheek. "Yes, I've got you. This time."

Wesley was nearly wild a week later when the charity show in Philadelphia called him away from Yelisa's side. She was doing very well and the doctor thought all danger of her losing the baby or of developing complications was past. Mercifully, the measures at the mine and plant had been sufficient to prevent any buildup of mercury in her system and she hadn't been exposed long enough the day of the accident to poison her.

Yelisa didn't really want him to go but she wanted even less to prevent him from going. Wesley was torn – he wanted to do the show, it was exciting and a good showcase for him and Prowess. It would also be a chance to renew acquaintances with some other musicians. But he hated to leave Yelisa. She needed him and he knew she didn't want him to go. If she had been well enough to go with him, it would have been fine. He did suggest that she go but she refused to travel in the wheelchair and the doctor insisted on her using it until after Christmas at least. They talked on the phone every night.

Wesley sat at the long desk-dresser in the hotel and dialed the number he knew best. Yelisa was waiting in the sitting room in her wheelchair, and answered promptly. She was full of Camille and her doings that night.

"She's so cute," Yelisa said happily. "She just babbles and laughs all the time she's awake now."

"And growing like a weed. And here I sit, three thousand miles away, missing it."

"How is Philly?"

"Colder'n a Montana well-digger's yah-yah."

Yelisa laughed. "There's a letter here for you from a lawyer in The Dalles."

"Open it and read it to me, will you?"

"Now there's a man with a spotless past. Are you sure you want me to?"

"Go ahead, you already know my most shameful secrets."

She laughed again and opened the envelope. She read, "'Masters, McElroy and Sondrup,' blah, blah, blah. 'Dear Mr. Callaghan, On behalf of my client, Mrs. Trudy Allen, I must inform you…'" She broke off, reading silently.

Wesley was alarmed. "Hello? Are you there, Yelisa?"

"Oh, Wesley, Trudy wants Camille. We're to surrender her by nine a.m. the twenty-first.

Wesley, we can't. She's ours. What are we going to do?"

"Yelisa..."

She interrupted him. "She can't do this. Wesley, we can't..."

Wesley broke in. "Yelisa..."

"She doesn't want the baby, Wesley. She just wants..."

Wesley became authoritative. "Yelisa. Listen to me. Are you listening/"

"Yes. Yes, I'm listening."

"Yeah. First, we're not going to panic. Okay?"

Yelisa took a deep breath. "Okay."

"Get in touch with the lawyer, what's his name? Benton. Find out what we ought to do. Take the letter with you and tell him the baby's mine."

"But, Wesley..."

"Yelisa, we'll talk when I get home. For now, do as I say. Will you?"

"I don't..."

"Yelisa. I know you're an executive and you're used to giving instructions instead of following them, but just this one time, do as I ask. Okay?"

"Okay." There was a smile in her voice a she added, "You should have left 'obey' in the marriage service."

"You wouldn't have been able to keep the promise anyway. I love you. Stay calm and I'll call you tomorrow."

"I love you, Wesley."

"Yeah. It's going to be all right."

"Good night."

"Good night."

Wesley pushed the cradle button down but sat with the receiver in his hand for a long time as if continued contact with the instrument could keep him closer to Yelisa.

Yelisa put her receiver down and picked up a framed snapshot of Wesley. She sat looking at it for a while then put it on her lap and wheeled herself into the nursery. She looked at the sleeping Camille and patted her very gently.

The next night Camille was on Yelisa's lap when the phone rang. She had carefully placed the baby so her kicking and arm-waving wouldn't strike any sore spots. She picked up the phone.

Wesley was lying on his bed in the dark with the draperies open so he could look out at the city lights.

"I saw Mr. Benton today," Yelisa said.

"And?"

"He thinks we can handle it with a suit in equity which is less formal than a trial."

"Good. What does it entail?"

'Well, Trudy has the right to demand a jury trial if she wants one. But, since the trial has to be here in Wheeler County because this is where the baby is, I don't really think she's going to demand a jury. She wants to sell us the baby and this is her way of jacking the price up."

"When will we have to go to court?"

Yelisa frowned. "You know what legalities are. It could drag on for months or years."

"No, it couldn't."

"What, then?"

"Tell Benton to get in touch with Trudy's lawyer and then set the date as soon as possible. I won't have you all upset just now."

"Okay, but it'll still be sometime early next year."

"Just tell him as soon as possible."

Yelisa grinned. "Right. Will expedite."

"What did the doctor say when you saw him this morning?"

"I'm fine. My incision is healing nicely. He's very pleased with me. At least he was."

"Was?" Wesley asked with a sinking heart.

"Well, I've been thinking about it and I've decided that our baby should be born at home. After all, Doc Hutchinson delivered me right here in the north gable room. He can deliver our baby here, too."

"Does he think it's a good idea?" He asked the question but he thought he already knew the answer.

"After I explained the alternative, he did."

"Yelisa," Wesley asked anxiously, "what was the alternative you gave him?"

"I told him you'd deliver it," she answered complacently.

"You lied," he exclaimed.

"Well, don't tell Doc that. Anyway, think about it and you'll see I'm right. What's the sense of carting me off to the clinic, probably in the middle of the night, when it's not necessary? I've got some books that tell how much better for the mother and the baby home delivery is. Everybody's happier."

"Yeah," Wesley said dryly, "I'm ecstatic."

Yelisa laughed. "How's the show shaping?"

"Fine. It's going to be a great show. Working with three other bands is pretty hectic, but we're going to raise some money for these folks."

"Well, it's a worthy cause," she said. "But I wish you were here with us right now. I'm sorry, I didn't mean to say that."

"I know. It's only two more days. I love you, Yelisa."

"I love you."

Chapter 16

Yelisa and Wesley spent a wonderful day driving out in the forest, finding the perfect Christmas tree. There was snow on the ground and the day was overcast and threatening. In spite of the weather, they were as happy as two people could well be. Wesley found a thickly branched fir that Yelisa said was too big. But he carried her to the tailgate to watch and cut the tree down anyway.

When they got home and took the tree out of the pickup and into the house, they found that Agnes had got all the Christmas decorations out. She insisted on giving them a hot toddy, with only a teaspoon of whiskey in Yelisa's, on account of the baby. Yelisa had always hated the taste of whiskey and she found an opportunity to pour hers into a potted fern. The three of them decorated the tree while Camille sat in her special little chair and watched, her eyes big and shining.

In the days that followed, packages mysteriously appeared under the tree. A couple of days before Christmas, Wesley's family arrived. The tree could scarcely contain the packages then, wide as it was. Yelisa liked Wesley's people at first sight. Denny hadn't come but she warmed to his parents and the twins at once.

Donna was a serene-faced woman, trim and cheerful. Brad's hair had slipped back to about the halfway mark, although his face was relatively unlined. Julie and Sara were dark and vivacious with a look of Wesley about them. They were identical twins, full of laughter and bubbling over with the joy of being young and alive.

Donna and Brad were satisfied with Yelisa. They had known that it would take an unusual woman to interest Wesley who had remained single for so long in the face of determined opposition, but they hadn't dared to hope for anyone as nice as Yelisa. And they could see at a glance that Wesley and Yelisa were deeply in love with one another.

Wesley's parents hadn't really accepted the fact that they had taken an infant who had no blood tie to either of them, though. They believed deep down that the baby was Wesley's and that he was shielding Yelisa. That belief worked in the baby's favor because it won her a place in their hearts as the truth never would have.

Julie and Sara loved Yelisa a soon as they met her. They admired her accomplishments at MacKenzie Mercury and they admired her poise and grace. Her personality attracted them because they knew very few women who had complete control over their own lives. They'd been indoctrinated into the philosophy of women's liberation, of course, and had observed their mother's traditional role of housewife from childhood. But it seemed to them that Yelisa had managed to combine the best of both worlds. And she'd done it without anger or scorn and without incurring anybody's wrath. She made it seem the most natural thing in the world. As it was. By Christmas Day both twins were firm friends with their new sister.

Wesley had been right about Julie and Sara and Camille. He and Yelisa had almost to forcibly take possession of their baby when they wanted to hold her. Agnes readily took to the twins and she warmed to Donna when Donna gently discouraged Yelisa from doing too much on grounds that she ought to rest for the baby's sake. Agnes and Donna got along quite well in the kitchen, exchanging recipes and stories of their children's growing-up years. By Christmas Day everyone was comfortable and happiness surrounded them like a down comforter.

Julie and Sara roused the house at seven Christmas morning by racing through the upstairs halls jingling some old sleigh bells they'd found in the stable. The sound was gentle and mellow, a good sound to awaken to if one had to be up as early as seven. The girls tended to Camille and gave her a bottle while Agnes and Donna made coffee and poured milk and prepared a simple breakfast.

Then the twins played Santa Claus, handing out the packages, piling their own in the middle of the floor where they had a wonderful time opening them after all the other packages had been handed out. Yelisa was sitting near the fireplace in her wheelchair. Wesley was on the floor at her side, holding Camille. Donna and Brad were on the sofa across the room. Jack was sitting beside Wesley, wagging his tail, taking in the sights and sounds of glee. There was a tide of wrapping paper and ribbons nearly knee-deep when Agnes rose and waded to the door.

"I've got things to see to in the kitchen," she said. "I'll get this mess later."

"You tend to the cooking," Wesley told her, "we'll get this mess. A good cook is much too valuable to waste on picking up wrapping paper."

Donna smiled at the twins who were admiring the cashmere sweaters that Wesley had given them, a turquoise one for Julie; a pale yellow one for Sara. She jumped up and followed Aggie, "May I help you?" she asked.

"You bet," was Aggie's answer.

The two older women left the room and Brad went to stand at the window. "It's starting to snow again," he said.

"Yippee!" Julie exclaimed. "Wesley, come out and help us make a snowman."

"We've never made a snowman," Sara added. "Come show us how."

"I've never made a snowman, either," Wesley said.

"I thought you knew how to do everything," Sara said accusingly.

"But you've lived in the north for years, Wes," Julie said, surprised.

"It isn't too often you get a cowboy out in the snow all by himself building a snowman," Wesley answered.

Sara nodded sagely. "Bizarre behavior, huh?"

Yelisa laughed. "Bizarre is right. I'd like to hear what the boys in the bunkhouse would have to say."

"Yeah," Wesley agreed.

Julie scrambled up. "Come on, Sara, let's put our new sweaters on and go play in the snow."

Sara followed her sister out and they raced noisily up the stairs.

Yelisa reached for the baby. "Let me have Camille, she's due for a bottle in a few minutes."

"She's such a prompt baby," Wesley said. "Every four hours, right to the minute, almost."

Wesley stood and put the baby on her lap. He wheeled them into the kitchen. When he came back, he stood beside his father, watching the big white flakes drift lazily down. The snow was about a foot deep and it was very beautiful outside in the morning light.

Brad smiled at Wesley. "Well, son, it's taken a long time."

"For me to settle down, you mean?"

Brad nodded.

"It was a lot of fun not to be settled, Dad."

"I guess it's natural for parents to want to see their offspring settled and secure."

"I know what you mean." Wesley looked out at the snowflakes. "A man gets lonesome."

"I don't think you need to worry about loneliness anymore. Your wife is quite a lady. It looks like you'll have a whole houseful of kids. But are you sure it's wise to keep traveling around like you do? Have you thought of Yelisa?"

"I've thought of very little else since the first minute I saw her."

"Everything's so good for you now. It wouldn't hurt you to make a little sacrifice and stay home with her. You could still write and publish. The real money's in publishing anyhow."

"The money's only part of it, though. My job is to write and perform music. Either by itself is not the whole job. It might become the whole job sometime. Right now it's not."

"It just seems to me that it wouldn't be much of a sacrifice on your part and she needs you."

Wesley put his hand on his father's shoulder. "It's all right, Dad. Yelisa and I don't believe in sacrifices."

The twins came down the stairs then, bundled up in sweaters, jackets, knitted caps and gloves. Wesley took his coat out of the front closet and went with them to help with the snowman. Jack gamboled about them as they rolled an enormous ball and positioned it in the middle of the lawn, topped it by a slightly smaller one and finished with the head. Yelisa wheeled herself out on the porch to watch and give the girls a red striped muffler and stocking cap to put on the snowman. She also had a carrot for his nose and a handful of black buttons for his mouth and eyes. Wesley suggested making a snowwoman upon which the girls began to pelt him with snowballs while Jack barked excitedly, racing around and hindering Wesley's efforts at retaliation. Yelisa laughed as her husband got well plastered with snow. He finally made a rush and tackled Sara. The twins were standing so close that when she want down, Julie fell, too. He rolled them thoroughly in the snow and they were laughing helplessly when Donna opened the front door.

"Dinner's nearly ready, you'd better come in now, children," she said and went back inside and shut the door.

Julie looked disgusted. "Don't parents ever quit thinking of their offspring as children?"

"Children!" Sara echoed. "Good grief!"

"If you don't want to sit in the corner for Christmas dinner," Wesley said, "you'd better hustle your bustles."

The two girls made faces at him and hurried up the steps and into the house, brushing the snow off each other as they went, Jack at their heels. Wesley joined Yelisa on the porch. He looked down at her face, so lovely and serene with her approaching motherhood.

"Is it a good Christmas for you?" he asked softly.

Yelisa was surprised that he needed to ask. "I'm loving every minute of it. It's wonderful to have a whole family again instead of just Agnes and one crabby sister."

Wesley tipped her face up to look into her eyes. He knelt and folded her in his arms and kissed her tenderly.

Chapter 17

It wasn't until mid-January that they were able to get a hearing with the judge. Yelisa was out of the wheelchair but still on crutches and her leg was still in a cast. The judge was an old family friend of the MacKenzies, the son of one of her father's closest friends. Yelisa wore a pale blue skirted maternity suit and noted with satisfaction that she looked very fragile and appealing. Wesley had protested when she suggested that he wear a business suit but Yelisa had insisted that the judge would think better of him than if he wore his customary jeans and western shirt. Seeing the judge, Wesley was glad he'd listened to his wife.

The lawyers and Tom Plank were also wearing business suits. The court clerk was a young woman who wore a pleated skirt and white blouse. Yelisa found Trudy less appropriately dressed but she was quite pleased with the effect, knowing that the judge was very stern with any kind of moral lapse on a woman's part. Trudy had chosen to get herself up like a high-priced whore. At least that's what the judge would think, Yelisa was sure. Trudy's dress was a black sheath, plainly made but embellished with lots of costume jewelry and closely fitted. Her hair was long, swept back from one side of her face and hanging nearly over her eye on the other side. With her four-inch heels, she looked very, very sexy. It might have worked with some judges.

Dr. Hutchinson and Mrs. Britton were in the spectators' seats behind Wesley and Yelisa. After the preliminaries, Trudy took the witness stand first and was sworn. Her lawyer, Mr. Sondrup, began to question her.

"Mrs. Allen," he said gently, "your daughter, the child known as Camille Callaghan, is two months old. That means she was conceived in mid-February last year. When did you first meet and become intimate with Mr. Callaghan?"

Trudy was very confident as she answered. "Sometime in the spring. Late April or early May."

"You were already two months pregnant when you met Mr. Callaghan?"

"Yes."

"So Mr. Callaghan is not the father of your child?"

"That is correct. He is not."

"Who is the father of your child, Mrs. Allen?"

"Philip Allen."

"Mrs. Allen, I'm sure the opposing counsel will bring this up so we might as well cover it first: You left Fossil some weeks ago and left your daughter behind. Was it your intention to abandon her?"

"No, of course not. I was distraught – not thinking clearly. I was on the verge of a nervous breakdown or I would never have done it. I know it was an awful thing to do, to leave her alone like that. But I had arranged for Mrs. Britton to take care of her. Mrs. Britton had promised to get the baby at ten o'clock. I should have waited to make sure. I blame myself bitterly for leaving her that night, but I'd given Mrs. Britton a hundred dollars and I thought that would ensure her taking care of the baby."

Mrs. Britton bounded in her seat indignantly and it was evident that she was having a hard time keeping herself from speaking her mind. When it was his turn, Wesley's lawyer, Mr. Benton, was quiet and calm and gave the impression that all he wanted was the truth, no matter what it was. He was deceptively gentle in his questioning of Trudy.

"Mrs. Allen, you've testified that a man named Philip Allen is the father of your baby. Mr. Allen is not in the courtroom today. Can you tell us why he is absent?"

"I don't know where he is. I couldn't get in touch with him."

"When you were last associated with Mr. Allen, did you inform him that you had conceived his child?"

"No, I didn't."

"But the child is the legitimate issue of yourself and your husband, Mr. Philip Allen?" Benton persisted.

"Phil and I aren't married," Trudy answered.

"But you call yourself Mrs. Allen?"

"Mrs. sounds better. There's no law against it."

"Assuredly not." Benton was still gentle. "Mrs. Allen, I have here a copy of the birth certificate you filed for your child. Please take it and read the name given as father."

Reluctantly, Trudy took it and looked at it. "Wesley Callaghan. But it isn't true!"

From the look on Sondrup's face, Yelisa — and the judge — gathered that this was the first he had heard of the birth certificate. Either he had overlooked the fact that there would be one or his client had lied to him and he hadn't bothered to check for himself. Tom Plant scowled at Trudy.

"Can you explain why you put Mr. Callaghan's name down as the father, if it isn't true?" asked Benton.

"I was confused and hurt. I didn't realize what I was doing."

"I see. Mrs. Allen, how do you earn your living?"

Sondrup objected. "Irrelevant, Your Honor."

The judge looked at Trudy thoughtfully. "I'll let it stand. The witness will answer the question."

"I'm a housewife."

Benton permitted himself to be surprised. "It was my understanding that you aren't married. Am I in error on that point?"

"I'm not married but I am Mr. Plank's housekeeper."

"You live in Mr. Plank's home and perform the duties and services of a housewife?"

"Yes." Evidently she thought this exchange just as damaging as Yelisa did because she turned directly to the judge and spoke passionately. "Listen, Your Honor, that baby's mine, not Wesley's. Whatever he says, he's not her father. But nobody denies that I'm her mother. Please, give her back to me." She began to cry. "I don't know why Wesley and his wife took my baby away from me but she's mine and I want her back. Don't they have enough without taking what's mine? They're rich and happy and they're going to have a baby of their own. Don't give them mine, too!"

The judge didn't appear to be much impressed with this plea. He asked if Benton had any further questions and, when he did not, dismissed Trudy from the witness stand. Sondrup put his hand on her arm and led her back to the table where Tom was sitting, frowning at her. Wesley was called to the stand and Benton began to question him.

When did you meet Mrs. Allen?"

"At a New Year's party a little more than a year ago."

225

Trudy jumped to her feet. "That's a lie! We didn't meet until..."

The judge banged his gavel and Sondrup took her by the arm and tugged. She glanced at Tom and sat down reluctantly. She whispered urgently to Sondrup and he shook his head.

Benton continued. "Do you remember the circumstances of that meeting, Mr. Callaghan?"

"Vividly. The party was given by an old friend of mine, Howard Siegel. It was at his home in Beverly Hills. I asked him who the gorgeous brunette was and he introduced me to Trudy."

Trudy shook her head vehemently but Tom and Sondrup kept her from interrupting again. When it was his turn to do the questioning, Sondrup tried to recover the ground he felt he'd lost by Trudy's emotionalism.

"Mr. Callaghan, you're a singer. Is that right?"

"Yeah."

"And because of the nature of your work, you spend a lot of time away from home?"

"I have a copy of my concert schedule here." Wesley handed a paper to Sondrup. "It shows the number of concert and travel days I've spent away from home since my daughter came to live with me. I'd like to say that it's my belief..."

Sondrup interrupted him. "Mr. Callaghan, your beliefs have no bearing on the question before this court. Now, isn't it true that when Mrs. Allen told you she was pregnant, you immediately, coldly and callously, denied that the child could be yours?"

"No, sir." Wesley glanced at Trudy. "I was delighted at the prospect of being a father."

Only Tom's hand squeezing her arm kept Trudy quiet and in her seat.

Sondrup continued, "Mr. Callaghan, are you aware of the consequences of perjury?"

"Not in detail. I have never needed that information."

The judge nearly smiled and Yelisa shook her head at Wesley but did give him a small smile.

"Please keep your answers responsive, Mr. Callaghan," Sondrup said. "Is it not true that when I requested your counsel to provide DNA samples from both you and the child known as Camille Callaghan, you refused?"

"Yes."

"Why was that? Why did you refuse to have a DNA analysis made?"

Wesley took a moment to frame his answer. "I thought it was unnecessary. Trudy and I both know that Camille is my daughter, so why bother?"

"Mr. Callaghan, isn't it true that you refused the DNA testing because you knew it would prove that you are not the child's father?"

"Absolutely not."

"Isn't it true that from whatever motive, spite or a desire to hurt my client because she left you, you decided to kidnap her child and keep her?"

Benton rose to his feet. "Your honor, I object. Nothing in the record shows any foundation for such a motive on the part of my client."

"Objection sustained," agreed the judge. "Keep your questions germane to the issue, Counselor."

Sondrup tried a couple more times to impugn Wesley's motive, but Benton successfully blocked him each time. Finally, he gave up and declared he had no further questions. Benton called Dr. Hutchinson to the stand. After he was sworn and had been asked a few questions designed to put the witness at ease, Benton got down to the nitty-gritty.

"Dr. Hutchinson, please describe the kind of blood test used to determine a child's paternity."

Doc Hutchinson described the various blood groups.

"Is this blood typing a conclusive test?"

"No, of course not," Doc answered. "For instance, if the child's blood is Type O or A, and the mother's is Type B, we know that a man with Type B blood cannot be the father. But if the man in question has Type A blood, he may be the baby's father."

"Have you typed Camille Callaghan's blood?"

"I have. It is Type A."

Benton paused for dramatic effect. "Have you typed Wesley Callaghan's blood?"

"I have. It is also Type A."

"So it's possible that Mr. Callaghan fathered the child, but not proved. Is that correct?"

"That is correct."

Sondrup, offered the opportunity to cross-examine the doctor, declined sourly. Benton called Mrs. Britton to the witness stand. Her testimony was given with many venomous glances at Trudy but Yelisa didn't think it hurt their cause too much.

In answer to a question from Benton, Mrs. Britton testified, "Trudy never told me she was going away and she never asked me to babysit. And she never give me no hundred dollars, either! I saw her and Tom leave that night but I never dreamt that she didn't take the baby with her."

"When you found the baby the next day, why did you call Mrs. Callaghan to come and get her?"

"She'd been giving Trudy money and paying her rent and Trudy told me time and time again that Wesley Callaghan was her baby's father and she was gonna make him pay."

Sondrup did his best but after that testimony, the decision was a foregone conclusion, although it wouldn't be official for a week or two after the judge considered the evidence. The legal courtesies were observed and court was adjourned. Yelisa was exhausted with the emotional turmoil and Wesley was tight-lipped as he opened the Mercedes door for her and then got behind the steering wheel.

"Oh, that Trudy," Yelisa said as they drove out of town. "What a liar that woman is."

"Don't knock it," Wesley told her. "I put in some pretty fair perjury myself. I think we convinced the judge that I'm Camille's father, though."

Yelisa smiled wanly. "Yes, circumstantial lying is so much more convincing than the truth with no particular bolstering. You think he'll give her to us?"

"I think he'd like to. But he may find the tradition of giving custody to the mother too strong for him."

"He can't. He mustn't."

"I hope he doesn't take too long handing down his decision," Wesley said, glancing at her anxiously.

"It's awful, having to wait."

"Yeah. You aren't very good at waiting, are you?"

About a week later, Wesley and Yelisa looked out at the beauty of the day and decided to take a walk. It was a balmy winter day, the kind that is sometimes as warm and mild as June. Yelisa was seven months pregnant and walking with a definite backward tilt. Wesley carried Camille, who at three months was a bright, happy baby. The trail they chose wound across a reasonably level stretch of forest to a creek.

Wesley helped Yelisa over a log and they sat down for a while to play with the baby and enjoy the peace of the woods.

"I wish to goodness we'd hear the outcome of that hearing. This waiting is driving me crazy," Yelisa said.

"Maybe there'll be news when we get back." Wesley remained calm and serene but it was mostly by act of will in order to keep Yelisa from going off the deep end. He thought that if he appeared to be worried or excited about it, she would fly right up in the air. And he'd taken Dr. Hutchinson's warnings about keeping her calm very seriously, although the danger had passed a few weeks after the accident.

"She's so sweet, Wesley. I couldn't bear to lose her now."

Wesley hugged them both. "I know."

She laughed. "Two more months and you'll have another one, Pop."

Wesley looked at her speculatively. "How many children do you actually want, Yelisa?"

"I never really thought about the number," she said.

"Think about it now," he urged.

Yelisa laughed again. "Afraid you can't keep up?"

"If you're going to break your legs and/or blow yourself up every time, I'm afraid you can't keep up," he countered.

The news finally came one day when Yelisa was at the mine. She stepped out of the elevator cage as Wesley stepped out of his pickup. He watched her in her floppy protective clothing. In order to get enough room to accommodate the baby, she'd had to use a man's size and roll up the legs and sleeves. He thought she looked like Dopey of Disney's Seven Dwarves. Yelisa knew he had news as soon as she saw him because he seldom came out to the mine for any reason. She hurried to him and he swooped her into his arms and off her feet. He kissed her and she took the envelope from him. He set her on her feet and she laughed up at him.

"She's ours," he said. "Camille's really ours. The judge has found that I'm her father and granted me custody."

"Oh, Wesley! I'm so relieved. It took so long, I was afraid."

"There's a catch, Yelisa. He granted Trudy visiting rights."

"Oh, no. He can't do that."

"I'm afraid he can. And has. She's allowed to see the baby one weekend a month and two weeks in the summer. She is also allowed a week at Christmastime, including Christmas Day."

"No. I won't have it. I'll call Mr. Benton now and get him to draw up something for Trudy to sign. We can't risk her taking the baby and not bringing her back. And God only knows what she'd learn during those visits."

"You think she'll sign it?"

"She'll sign."

A few days later, Yelisa and Trudy met on a dirt road in the middle of the wheat country. Barren-looking, snow-blown hills were all around them, with no houses in sight. The two women were standing between their cars and Yelisa was holding a manila envelope, a paper and a pen. She hadn't told Wesley about the meeting, feeling sure he would insist on accompanying her and thinking it would be best to keep it just between her and Trudy. She eyed Trudy with a good deal of dislike but tried to keep it from showing.

"Look, Trudy, let's stop playing games. You don't want Camille, even for a weekend now and then. You want to sell her and I'm ready to pay."

"I suppose, with no witnesses, I might as well level. The only reason I didn't abort her was that I thought she would be a lever to use on Wesley. His taking up with Miss Rich Bitch was a Godsend to me. And you wanting 'his baby.' Did you bring the money? All of it?"

Yelisa held the envelope up. "It's here." She handed Trudy the pen and paper. "Sign first."

Trudy signed and Yelisa took the paper and gave Trudy the envelope. Trudy laid the stacks of bills out on the hood of her car.

"It's all there," Yelisa said.

Trudy laughed derisively. "Every day I'll think of you with the two o'clock feeding and the dirty diapers and I'll laugh. God, how I'm gonna laugh. She really isn't Wesley's." Trudy was still laughing when she got in her car and drove away.

Yelisa smiled to herself. "I know," she said.

Chapter 18

The winter passed in long hours of satisfying work and long evenings of precious, quiet joy and love. Wesley wrote two of the best works of his career that winter. Eventually, the public recognized the one but the other went practically unnoticed. Monte and the boys spent six weeks at Dightman's while they worked on the music for the new album. Wesley and Monte collaborated on three songs and Jimmy came up with one that they included.

Yelisa went to the office five days a week but she shortened her hours to eight or nine instead of the ten to twelve she'd been putting in. She found that she'd been doing a lot of work that could be delegated to Faye or Eldon Richards. She was pleased with Eldon, he was good at the work and he liked it. She would be able to leave him in charge now and again while she traveled with Wesley.

She loved the evenings when she and Wesley could play with Camille. The baby grew at a rate that amazed Yelisa although Wesley said she was right on schedule. It still surprised Yelisa that Wesley was so knowledgeable about babies. And that he enjoyed Camille and parenthood as much as she did.

After Camille went to sleep, Wesley often went back to work with his guitar or on the piano, getting some of the music that permeated his being shaped into songs. Yelisa loved to sit with him then, reading or sewing or just listening. She wasn't much help, partly because she was totally uncritical and partly because she had no wish to encroach on his work. Sometimes he'd ask her about the way the lyrics sounded or if she liked a phrase of music but mostly he was content just to have her there.

One afternoon in mid-April, Wesley was sitting on the front steps playing with a new melody on the guitar. The snow had gone and the yard was looking dreary and muddy but there was a softness in the air that promised better things to come soon. It was almost too chilly to be outside but he'd needed to get out into the fresh air. When Yelisa drove in he stopped playing and put the guitar aside.

He held her for a moment and she smiled and kissed him. Then he opened the door for her and took her coat. He steered her into the music parlor and she sat on the sofa and put her feet on the coffee table. Wesley stood looking down at her sternly.

"I thought you were only going to go look at the charts and come right back," he said.

Yelisa smiled guiltily. "I meant to. But Eldon asked me a question and one thing led to another."

"Yeah. In another five minutes, I'd have been out looking for you."

"I think I'd better not go to the office until this infant is out where I can leave him in the nursery."

"Thank God, the girl does have some sense."

"Did you finish your song today?"

"No, I was too worried about you."

Yelisa grinned up at him, completely unrepentant. "That's right, blame it all on me."

"Actually, I did finish it. Like to hear it?"

"Yes, please."

Wesley went to the piano to sing and play a soft and tender love song. The music was sweet and very moving.

Yelisa was enchanted. "Wesley, it's exquisite."

He left the piano to kneel beside her. "It's one of the best things I've done."

"I thought you needed one more hard-driving rocker-type number."

"I'm saving that for a surprise. The boys'll be here again next week to rehearse and get the arrangements down."

"I hope this baby's out in the open by then."

Wesley put both hands on her belly. He could feel the baby moving and he imagined the tiny body with its miniature fists and knees stretching and turning.

"He's an active little devil, isn't he?" Wesley asked with pride.

"He is that. He has just kicked hell out of me all day long. I'm going upstairs and relax until dinner. Camille might be awake, let's go play with her."

Agnes was just finishing changing Camille when Wesley and Yelisa entered the nursery. She looked up and smiled at them. Jack was watching the baby, wagging his tail.

Wesley looked at him and frowned. "You women have ruined my dog."

At the sound of Wesley's voice, Jack came to stand looking up at him. Wesley bent down to pet him.

"Nonsense," Yelisa said. "Look how he comes when he hears his master's voice."

Agnes picked Camille up. "Come to take her away?"

"If you don't need her for the moment," Yelisa said.

Camille held her hands out to Wesley and he took her. They went into the sitting room and Jack went with them. Yelisa stretched out on the sofa while Wesley and Camille sat on the floor to play. Yelisa got a funny, surprised look on her face and moved both hands to cradle her unborn child. She watched Wesley and Camille for a few minutes then her face twisted with pain.

Wesley propped the baby up and let go momentarily. "Look, she can sit up all by herself."

"That's more than old mom can do, I think."

"Yelisa?" Wesley put Camille down on her stomach and went to his wife.

"I think you'd better call Doc Hutchinson and warn him tonight's the night."

"Wait right there," Wesley said needlessly. He picked Camille up and hurried to the door. "Don't try to move. I'll be back in a minute."

"All right. It won't be here for hours, you know."

He looked at her suspiciously. Although he and Yelisa had had training from Doc Hutchinson and they knew what to do even if they couldn't get the doctor, Wesley hadn't forgotten the shock he'd got when he came home in December to find Yelisa placidly feeding an infant. He'd known it was months too soon but for just a moment he'd thought she'd done something spectacular. "I'm not counting on it," he said, and disappeared through the door.

He was back in a couple of minutes with Agnes. He stooped and brushed his lips across Yelisa's forehead. Agnes hurried to open the bedroom door.

"Is he coming?" Yelisa asked.

"Yes, but not right away," Wesley told her.

Yelisa twisted with pain. "Why not? Wesley, I don't think this baby's going to be long in coming."

"The damn fool is clear to hell and gone over to Hardman," Wesley said savagely. "Some fool of a cowboy got himself kicked and insisted he had to have Doc Hutchinson patch him up. His nurse will be right out, though."

"That's good." Yelisa was relieved. "Mrs. Franson can deliver the baby if she has to."

Wesley picked her up and carried her into the bedroom. He put her very carefully on the bed and knelt beside her, holding her hand in both of his.

Agnes shooed him out. "We won't be needing you for a while, Wesley. Go down and boil some water or make some coffee or play with Camille until I call you. Or until the doctor gets here."

Wesley rose reluctantly. "I think Camille went to sleep already," he said plaintively. "All right, I'll stay out of the way." He went out the door but stuck his head back in immediately. "Do you need any boiling water or is that just to get me out of the way?"

Yelisa smiled at him. "Will you stay out of the way without boiling the water?"

"I'll try."

"You'd better boil the water."

He went back to check on Camille and found her lying on her back, her eyes wide open, watching the door. She smiled when she saw him and he picked her up to her intense delight. She looked so tiny and helpless and sweet. And very soon she'd have a brother or sister. Wesley's eyes misted and his heart seemed to swell with the beauty of new life. Jack sat beside him, knowing something momentous was happening but not knowing what. He watched Wesley worriedly. Wesley went downstairs, Jack at his heels. He was too nervous to stay still. Doc Hutchinson had assured him that Yelisa's delivery would be simple and normal and there was nothing to worry about. But Wesley knew that things could go wrong in childbirth and if they did, Yelisa would be the one to suffer most. He needed to be doing something, to keep himself busy so he wouldn't think unbearable thoughts.

He put Camille in her little seat and strapped her in. Jack sat down near the baby, dividing his attention between her and Wesley. Wesley found the big canning kettle and filled it with water, explaining to Camille and Jack what he was doing and why. Then he stood and watched it, waiting for it to boil. But there is very little entertainment value in watching water heating up so he made a pot of coffee. That didn't take long, either. The doorbell rang and he scooped up Camille, baby seat and all, and hurried to answer it, Jack following.

Mrs. Franson smiled serenely at him and assured him that the doctor would be there soon. She'd left a message with Mrs. Hutchinson who expected the doctor back directly. He took Mrs. Franson upstairs and she shooed him out of the bedroom and closed the door firmly behind him. He sat on the floor of the sitting room with his back against the sofa, holding Camille on his lap. Jack paced from Wesley to the bedroom door and back again. He stopped and whimpered, looking at Wesley for reassurance.

"It's all right, Jack," Wesley said. He stroked the collie's golden coat. "Yelisa's all right, boy."

Jack looked doubtful but flopped down beside his master with his chin on his paws, alternately watching Wesley and Camille and the door. After awhile, Agnes came out and told him everything was fine. She went downstairs for some coffee for the nurse. She found the canning kettle boiling merrily and smiled as she turned the burner under it off. The coffee Wesley had made was about twice as strong as coffee ought to be so she poured it out and made a fresh pot.

She carried three mugs of coffee upstairs and paused to give Wesley one.

"Camille went to sleep so I put her in her crib," he said.

"Good. She should be good for several hours. Here, I brought you some coffee."

Wesley took a mug. "Was the water boiling?"

"Oh, yes. I turned the burner off. If the doctor needs sterile water, you certainly made enough."

"That was my intention."

Telling Jack to stay, Wesley set his coffee mug down and followed Agnes into the bedroom. He pulled a chair up to the bed and sat down, taking Yelisa's hand. She smiled at him and he smiled back.

"How's it going?" he asked softly.

"Fine. Where's Camille?"

"She's asleep. I left all the doors open so I can hear her if she wakes up."

"Good."

She squeezed his hand when a pain hit her and he was surprised at how strong her grip was. When she had been in labor about four hours, Dr. Hutchinson arrived. Aggie went downstairs to open the door and bring him up. He sent Wesley out of the bedroom. Wesley protested but the doctor was adamant.

"Like as not, you'd faint and we're going to have our hands full with your wife and baby. We can't contend with you, too. We'll call you just as soon as the baby's born."

Wesley went. Actually, he and Yelisa had agreed weeks earlier that he would not be present during the baby's actual birth. He was terribly afraid he would faint or make a fool of himself and Yelisa was afraid seeing her giving birth would forever destroy their romance. So Wesley stood outside the bedroom door and tried to hear what was going on. He could only hear an occasional murmur and sharp yelp. Then silence that seemed to go on forever. He started at an infant's sudden wail of protest. The doctor came out and nearly bumped into Wesley. He closed the door behind himself.

"Is she all right?" Wesley demanded.

"She's fine," the doctor answered heartily. "A good strong woman. You could have delivered the child yourself, Wesley."

Wesley was still rigid with the suspense. "The baby?"

"You have a fine healthy daughter. Nearly eight pounds if your scales are right."

A few minutes later the door opened and Mrs. Franson came out.

Yelisa called to him. "Wesley? Come in. Come and meet your daughter."

Wesley went into the bedroom and Agnes went out, closing the door behind her. Yelisa was propped up against the pillows, her hair was damp and tousled and she looked exhausted but her smile was radiant. Wesley knelt at her side and they both looked at the baby wrapped in a receiving blanket and cradled in Yelisa's arm.

"Thank God," Wesley said fervently. "It got so quiet I was afraid things were going wrong."

"Were you expecting screams and hideous shrieks?"

"I guess I was."

"After I explained about home delivery being so peaceful and happy?" Yelisa smiled at him. "Isn't she beautiful?"

"She's lovely. She even has hair."

"You're not disappointed she's a girl?"

"I'll forgive you."

"I'll give you a son next time."

"Next time?" Wesley was horrified. "You don't think I'm going through all this again, do you?"

Yelisa looked at him and smiled angelically. "I think you will."

Three months later the stage was set in the middle of an arena. It was rigged with an extensive stack and several men were at various control boards, putting the finishing touches on the sound system. It was nearly show time.

The dressing room was a motor home with "Wesley Callaghan and Prowess" emblazoned on the sides. The band's dressing room was a bus converted to a motorized dormitory. There was a crackle of excitement as the band laughed and bantered while they were getting ready to perform.

Agnes was cleaning the high chair. Camille, at seven months, was crawling toward the door. Three-month-old Kelly was sitting on Yelisa's lap and Wesley was in front of the mirror combing his hair. He saw Camille and went to scoop her out of the doorway, shutting the screen tightly. There was a perfunctory knock on the door and the tour manager entered the room with one of the local disc jockeys. The DJ was a little nervous about meeting such a big star and trying hard not to show it. Yelisa put Kelly in her bassinet and came forward to stand beside Wesley.

The tour manager performed introductions. "Yelisa, Wesley, I'd like you to meet Shawn Hatfield. Shawn's got the most-listened-to show in the area."

Wesley shook hands with the DJ and Yelisa smiled at him. "I'm real glad to know you, Shawn," Wesley said. "This is Agnes Pratt and those are my daughters, Camille and Kelly. Kelly is the younger one."

Agnes turned to nod at the DJ.

"That was a nice spread 'Country Cousins Magazine' ran last month," Shawn said.

"They were real good to us," Wesley agreed. "I thought the pictures of the rehearsal were especially good."

Yelisa nodded. "You could almost hear the music."

They left the motor home to walk slowly to the backstage area.

"Is it true that you delivered your younger daughter, Wesley?" Shawn asked.

Wesley shuddered. "No. No. I don't have the guts to go in for the really rough stuff."

"You rescued a man from an enraged bull once," Yelisa reminded him.

"Compared to delivering babies, bulls are kindergarten heroics."

"According to the magazine article, your daughters are only four months apart," Shawn said, a little brashly to cover his nervousness. "I know a lot of my listeners would like to know about that spacing. Would you give me something to quote?"

"Yeah," Wesley said solemnly. "See, up there in eastern Oregon, there's just a small population. So there aren't many people to bug you. And the fact is, although I'm married to Yelisa, I keep a harem on the side."

Shawn was startled. "A harem?" Then he realized that Wesley was pulling his leg. "Oh, you're kidding, of course. Okay, I can do something with that."

The band was standing near the stage steps, waiting for Wesley and Shawn. The guys and Shawn filed onto the stage and took their places. Wesley took Yelisa's hand; in the other she held a microphone.

Shawn was introducing them. "Tune in from seven to midnight, Wednesday through Sunday and listen to the tracks these great musicians have cut. And now it gives me great pleasure to introduce my very good friends, Wesley Callaghan and Prowess!"

Tumultuous applause went up on all sides. Wesley and Yelisa walked out onto the stage and shook hands with Shawn. Shawn left the stage and Wesley stepped in close to the floor mike.

"Thank you," he said. The applause continued and he said it again. And yet a third time. "Thank you, we appreciate it. Listen, I've got a real treat for you. My lovely wife has consented to help me out with this first number."

The applause was renewed as Yelisa bowed to the audience. Wesley dropped his hand in signal to the band. Barney struck a brilliant riff on his drums; the keyboard and guitars came into play and Yelisa began to sing. The music was pure joy made audible in a glittering cascade of sound. Wesley sent a dazzling smile to Yelisa and joined his voice with hers.

ABOUT THE AUTHOR

Barbara J. Olexer

Barbara is a fourth-generation Oregonian. She has written more than twenty books and screenplays. Her first published book was *The Enslavement of the American Indian*, a nonfiction account of a little-known segment of American history.

Her formative years were mostly spent in a small farming town and a backwoods logging camp. It was while she lived in the logging camp that she attended Wheeler County High School in Fossil, Oregon. Barbara's life has been a tapestry of changes as she has lived and worked in small Oregon towns and some of the country's biggest cities, such as San Francisco, Hollywood, Baltimore, and Washington, D.C. Her heart remains in rural Oregon.

While her two sons and five grandchildren live in Oregon, Barbara lives in Columbia, Maryland, with her husband and pug dog, Chad.

www.ingramcontent.com/pod-product-compliance
Lightning Source LLC
Chambersburg PA
CBHW051635260626
47170CB00004B/1185